OLYMPUS ACADEMY

THE DEMON DEMIGOD

ELIZA RAINE

Editors: Kyra Wilson, Brittany Smith

1

'Oh Gods, I'm so sorry!' I squealed as the tidal wave crashed over Dasko, then whirled away noisily down the drain in the middle of the room. Dasko kept his eyes closed a moment, standing still as water dripped from his sodden clothes. Snickers rang out behind me and I felt my face heat.

'Pandora, please stay after class,' the professor said eventually. I nodded, stomach sinking. 'You're not in trouble,' he added, looking at me as he shook out his wet sleeves. 'But we need to put in some extra time to practice your water powers.'

'Yes, professor,' I mumbled. I headed to the back of the room and leaned against the cool stone wall, watching as the other students took it in turns to create little whirlpools in their palms or small waves that danced out of the water wall at the back of the room, then dissipated harmlessly at their feet. Arketa shrieked and leaped backward as Kiko's wave got too close to her pretty heeled shoes. I looked down at my own soggy, stained red

Converse. Dad and Mandy's faces flashed in my mind. It had been four months since I had seen my family. Four months since I had joined Olympus Academy. And although I now had power, I didn't know what to do with it. The restless feeling that had dominated my life before coming to Olympus hadn't lessened with the unlocking of my Titan powers. It had *grown*.

Dasko said that being a descendant of Oceanus and having epic water powers was always going to be tricky when living in an underwater school. I was constantly aware of the ocean around us, its churning, changing, enormous power bubbling under my skin all the time. I dreamed of it at night - dreamed that I *was* the water, racing free around an endless globe, giving life to everything I passed. Some of the creatures I saw I couldn't even describe - and never saw again. Some were just like the ones I'd grown up seeing in aquariums back home, like the turtle family that Zali and I swam with every day now. I couldn't communicate with them like Zali could, with actual words, but I could sense their mood and their intent. I knew if they were unsettled, happy or in danger.

The gong sounded and the students began filing out of the water elemental classroom. I stayed where I was, ignoring Arketa's nasty comment as she strolled past.

'With any luck you'll drown yourself, Titan scum,' she sneered. 'Titan girl' had been upgraded to 'Titan scum' for a little while now. I didn't want her words to her affect me, but I still just couldn't understand why she hated me so much. Icarus said it was best to ignore her, so that's what I was trying to do. He wasn't in my water classes anymore though, he just worked with air element now, so I had to put up with her on my own.

'Pandora, you need to work harder on this. If it gets back to Zeus that you can't control your powers-' Dasko started, but I cut him off, rolling my eyes.

'I'll get thrown out of the academy. I know, I know. I *am* trying.'

'Then try harder. Now, make a small wave from the wall. No higher than three feet,' he instructed me. I stared at waterfall wall, easily slipping my conscious into the flowing water. I pulled out a wave, slowly, cautiously. I drew it from the wall towards me, feeling the gentle flowing power growing. The press of the ocean around me grew, the heaving mass of energy calling to me. I shouted a curse as the wave leaped, drenching me from head to foot.

'I can't do it with the sea all around me!' I yelled, my frustration turning to anger.

'Yes, you can Pandora. You just need to practice controlling the feeling. Practice not letting it overtake you.' Dasko's voice was calm and his dark eyes settled on mine.

'Fine,' I said through gritted teeth after a pause. I tried again. And again, and again. I lost control of the wave every time. Eventually Dasko sighed and told me to stop.

'It's nearly dinner time. I'll see you tomorrow,' he said.

'I'm sorry,' I mumbled. 'I really am trying.'

'I know, Pandora. You'll get there,' he said with a smile.

I hoped he was right.

. . .

I told my friends about drenching Dasko in front of the whole class as soon as we sat down in our usual spot for dinner.

'Practice makes perfect. I'm sure you'll get there,' said my roommate Zali, characteristically optimistic. I gave her a warm smile.

'How are your fire classes going?' Tak asked me as we piled mashed potato onto our plates at dinner. I looked sideways at Icarus.

'Umm, alright, I guess,' I answered vaguely.

'I really like the new professor. He's helping me loads with Telekinesis.'

'Do you not think there's anything... off about him?' I asked carefully.

'Like what?' Tak asked, his eyebrows drawing together in a frown.

Like being a dangerous red-eyed demon, I thought but I just shrugged.

'I agree with Dora,' said Icarus. 'There's something strange about him.'

'Coming from you, that's quite an accusation,' said Gida, the satyr. I watched Icarus tense for a moment at the teasing, then relax, an easy smile crossing his face as his massive black wings rustled behind him.

'Well, at least I'm not half goat,' he said, with a sideways look at the satyr.

'Being half-goat has many advantages, I'll have you know,' Gida replied indignantly. I zoned out as they started comparing wings to hooves. My friends had accepted Icarus as easily as they had accepted me, and it warmed my heart to see him smiling and chatting with them. When we were alone, at the top of the pegasus tower and sharing stolen kisses in the twilight, he would talk non-stop about the places he wanted to visit and the realms he wanted to see. His excitement was infectious and so different to the moody, guarded boy I'd met before. The more time I spent with him, the more I realized how different, how incredible he was. I wanted so badly to ask him about the file I'd seen, about where he had been trapped and whether that was why he was so driven by being free, but I knew he would be furious with me for prying. He was finally opening up, and I had no intention of getting in the way of that, much as I burned to know about his past.

Professor Neos was another problem entirely. Every time Icarus or I had tried to tell Dasko about his glowing red eyes and our suspicion that he was the red demon that I had inadvertently let out of Oceanus's box, the teacher had stared at us in confusion and told us he couldn't understand our language. So we were trying to work out what to do about it on our own. Neos taught Fire and Earth elements, along with Telekinesis, which was only available to students who excelled at Telepathy. I hadn't made the grade, but Tak was doing great with it, now levitating salt and pepper pots towards other people's heads at every available opportunity.

I only saw Professor Neos in Fire class, and at least once every lesson I was positive he gave me a flash of those red eyes on purpose. I was desperate to just ask him outright if he was the demon, but Icarus said we had to be smarter about it. I could see where he was coming from. I mean, I didn't have a clue what we'd do if he actually said that yes, he *was* the demon. Besides, we were a full month into the new semester and nothing bad had happened. Yet.

After dinner the main temple transformed into the library and we settled ourselves on our usual couch. Icarus had to sit up on the back of it so that his wings could hang over unhindered, but he didn't seem to mind. I sat in front of him on the squishy cushion, his booted feet either side of me, and as Tak started setting up a dice game Roz sauntered over to us.

'Can I play, Tak?' she asked sweetly, with a slight glance at me and Icarus.

'Course you can,' he beamed at her. I looked at Zali, knowing she didn't like Roz. Tak and the pink-haired girl had danced together *a lot* at the last dance night, but this was the first time she'd approached us as a group in the library.

Zali looked straight back at me, her amber eyes flashing.

'Do you want to play something else?' she asked me.

'Sure,' I said, awkwardly, as Roz sat on a cushioned stool opposite Tak. 'What did you have-'

'Roz, what are you doing with these losers?' Arketa's voice cut across my words.

'Playing dice,' Roz shrugged, looking up at Arketa, Filis and Kiko. They all sneered in unison.

'You'll catch something,' said Filis, nose wrinkling.

'Don't be stupid, Filis,' Roz said and picked up the two

dice Tak had put in front of her. 'Do I roll first?' she asked him. Tak nodded as Filis went bright red.

'Did you just call me stupid?' she hissed. Arketa's face had darkened, anger dancing in her eyes.

'No, I said the idea of catching something from these people was stupid.' Roz looked up at the three girls. 'Unless you want to play, go away,' she said. My mouth fell open slightly. The last thing I had expected from somebody as popular as Roz was for her to take our side over Arketa's crowd. Arketa's lips pinched shut as Filis spluttered, and then she whirled on her heel, storming off without a word. Kiko paused a moment, gave the table a pointed look, then followed after her as it crashed over, the dice tumbling across the floor and under the couch.

'She's really, really good at Telekinesis,' grumbled Tak as he got on his hands and knees to gather them back up.

'Yeah, I can see that!' laughed Roz, and dropped down beside him. I looked at Zali and felt a pang of pity at the expression on her face as she watched them hunt for the dice together.

'You didn't seem to enjoy this evening?' I said to her as we closed the door to our dorm room later that night.

'Well it was hard to get a word in, with Roz taking over so much,' Zali answered shortly.

'She did take over a bit,' I agreed, secretly thinking that she hadn't at all. 'But it was great watching her put Filis in her place, wasn't it?'

'I guess so,' Zali answered, sitting down hard on her bed.

'I'm sensing you still don't like her,' I said slowly.

'I just don't trust her,' Zali scowled.

'We'll keep an eye on her,' I said, as reassuringly as I could. I thought it was highly likely that her dislike of Roz was connected to how much she *did* like Tak, but as she clearly wasn't ready to talk about it I decided to keep my mouth shut for a change.

2

As soon as I was sure Zali was asleep I crept back out of bed. I was at the base of the pegasus tower in minutes, the water surrounding the dome a gloomy deep blue above me. I got in the hauler, shifting impatiently from foot to foot as it zoomed upwards. I took a deep breath as the cool air hit my face when I reached the top, then jogged down the corridor towards the stables. I stopped when I reached Peto's stall, seeing Icarus sat on the walkway, his legs dangling over the edge and his huge black wings either side of him. Even though he'd had the wings for over a month now, they still took my breath away sometimes.

'Fancy seeing you here,' I said with a smile as I slowed. He climbed to his feet as he turned to me, pushing his hair back from his face and smiling back.

'I heard a pretty girl visits her pegasus some nights,' he muttered. Thrills rippled through me as I looked into his piercing green eyes and I stepped close to him.

'Is that right?' I whispered.

'It sure looks like it,' he answered, and kissed me under the moonlight.

'You know, we're going to get caught up here soon enough,' Icarus said a while later as I brushed Peto. The pegasus whinnied happily as I ran the coarse-bristled brush across his flank.

'Nah. I don't think anybody cares. Besides, we're not causing any trouble.'

'Hmmm.'

'Icarus, what are we going to do about the demons?'

He sighed. Our conversation turned to this every time we were alone and we still didn't have an answer.

'I don't know. Can you talk to Nix again?'

'Yeah. I have Magical Objects class tomorrow,' I said. But so far the phoenix hadn't provided any useful advice on the matter. 'I can't help feeling it's only a matter of time. The poem talked about spilling blood. I don't want us to act too late.'

'But we don't know where to start,' he protested.

'Yes, we do. Neos.'

'Dora, if he really is a demon, then he is the most dangerous thing in the academy. You must never be alone with him.' Icarus's eyes flashed fiercely as he spoke.

'If he wanted to hurt us he would have already! Not patiently taught students Telekinesis and Fire magic. No, he's up to something else. He's showing us his red eyes on purpose - he wants us to talk to him.' I was absolutely sure that what I was saying was true.

'Pandora, please.'

'Please what?' I looked at Icarus. 'We have to do something, we can't just wait for the demons to start killing people!' He flinched at my words, his wings fluttering behind him.

'Just don't do anything alone. Make sure I'm with you,' Icarus said eventually.

I rolled my eyes.

'I can handle myself, you know,' I said, feeling the power of the ocean below us hum through me at my words, as though reinforcing them.

'I know you can. It's one of the things I like best about you,' Icarus said quietly. I straightened and looked him in the eyes. 'I just think we're better as a team,' he said. My heart swelled in my chest. He was right. We were.

I awoke late the next morning and had to race to the showers before pulling on my swimsuit and bolting down to the pool.

My timetable for my second semester was simpler than it had been before I unlocked my powers. Now, my first class every day was swimming or flying and my last class was Water magic with Dasko. I still had one class each of Olympus Geography, History of Mythology and Ancient Language, along with Swords and Archery, but I no longer had Shifting, Telepathy, Electricity, Earth or Air. My only new class was Advanced Magical Objects. I still got to spend time with Nix's feather, but I also got to test other objects for magical powers, and Professor Fantasma promised we would be looking at cursed objects soon.

'Look, they're here already!' Zali called to me as I jogged to the pool edge. Miss Alma gave me a stern look.

'Sorry I'm late,' I muttered quickly, and slid into the water. I felt weightless instantly, the strength of the liquid supporting my body. My connection to the water meant I could swim for hours without tiring, the currents carrying me when my limbs no longer wanted to. But I could still only hold my breath for about four or five minutes. And short of growing gills, I couldn't see how that would change.

I swam quickly up to Zali, who was pointing at the family of turtles on the other side of the dome, twenty feet away. The littlest one wriggled excitedly as we waved.

'Class! I want you to race to get the red flag from the marker out there,' called Miss Alma loudly. We all followed her pointed arm to look out at the glowing red flag fifty feet out in the ocean beyond. 'Zali, you needed to do the distance twice before you can take it or there's no competition,' the teacher added. We all lined up against the wall of the pool. This was advanced swim class, so there were only ten of us, Arketa included.

'On your marks,' called Miss Alma. Arketa shot me a nasty look and my skin fizzed with adrenaline. I wanted to beat her.

'Get set...' I glared back at her, then focused on the red flag out in the sea.

'Go!' I pushed off the tiles hard, propelling myself through the pool. I took a massive breath in just before I reached the dome, then popped through it, relishing the cold water rushing over my head. Zali streaked past me, iridescent purple flashing in her tail as it whipped through the water ahead of me. I kicked my legs, willing the water around me to push me faster and felt it respond, a tight current beginning to whirl around me. My hair flew back from my face as I started to zoom towards the flag. I felt a tug on my ankle and jerked my head around. Arketa was hanging on to my foot, the strength of my current pulling her along with me. She gave me a nasty smile and I kicked my foot, trying to dislodge her. She pulled hard though, dragging herself forwards, then used her own water power to surge herself forwards, and past me. I growled, bubbles escaping my mouth, and kicked hard after her. For half a moment I considered using my power to pull her back, but the thought of the wave crashing over Dasko rang through my mind. What if I lost control and drowned her? At the thought, I felt the current I was riding in spin sharply. Panic crept around me as I concentrated on the ocean but it was too late. The current began to swirl downwards, dragging me in a spiral with it. I closed my eyes and forced myself into the water, commanding it to stop with everything I had. It slowed, mercifully, and when I opened my eyes again I was treading water ten feet below the others. And I looked up just in time top see Arketa snatch the red flag from the marker half a second before Zali reached it. A burning stab in my chest accompanied the flash of disappointment I felt, reminding me that I needed air. I kicked angrily back towards the pool, mentally cursing my inability to control my power.

'Next time,' Zali said with a shrug when my head broke the surface. My annoyance must have shown on my face because she put her hand on my shoulder and smiled. 'Don't let her ruin your day,' she said. I sighed, threw a glare at Arketa's smug face, and tried to push the anger away.

Miss Alma congratulated Arketa on her win, and we were allowed to swim as partners for the rest of the class. Zali and I headed straight out towards the turtles. Between trips back to the pool for air she screwed her face up in concentration, trying to communicate with them, whilst I tumbled around in little somersaults with the baby one until I was dizzy.

My next class was Magical Objects, and I was looking forward to talking to Nix again. I *knew* I was going to have to say something to Neos soon. I couldn't keep the need to know if he really was the red demon inside much longer.

'Nix,' I said, cradling his feather and settling down on a cushion between the bookshelves.

'Oh gods. You're hyper today,' his irritated voice replied.

'I lost a swimming race to Arketa because she cheated and I can't control my power,' I said.

'You shouldn't be losing races in the water. You're the most powerful Oceanus descendant I've ever come across. You must practice more.'

I rolled my eyes.

'Everyone keeps saying practice, and I am. But just doing the same thing over and over again leads to the same results over and over again,' I sighed.

'Then you're not doing it right.'

'Great. That's really helpful.'

The phoenix didn't reply.

'Nix, I want to talk to Professor Neos.'

'You talk to him every week in fire class.'

'I mean, about being a demon.'

'And are you just going to ask him? What will you do if he is the red demon?' The bird's voice was dry and cynical.

'Ask him what he wants with the academy,' I said, indignantly. 'He's obviously nothing like the sea monster we fought. And he hasn't spilled any blood yet.'

'That we know of,' added Nix. I swallowed.

'My point is, I think he wants me to acknowledge him. Maybe he just needs something from the school and he'll be on his way.'

'And you're deducing this from your extensive experience of demons, are you?' Sarcasm dripped from his words.

'I'm deducing it from common sense,' I snapped back.

'Pandora, you haven't even studied demons yet. If a god as powerful as Oceanus decided this one needed to be locked up, then there's a very good reason.'

'But the poem said, *But for the hero who can handle the gore, Is finally a chance to end this bloody war.* What if we're supposed to make peace with the demons?'

'The previous line said, For every drop of blood they spill, They will become much harder to kill. *Study demons, Pandora. Learn what you can first. Do not approach him.'*

I sighed.

'Fine.'

3

A fter lunch I had History of Mythology with Dasko, so I decided to try to follow Nix's advice.

'Professor Dasko?' I raised my hand as soon as I sat down with the rest of my year. We were all in one class now that Icarus and I had caught up.

'Yes, Pandora,' he said, giving me a look. I was often the first to ask questions in class.

'Instead of the Olympian family tree, which is very interesting, please can we learn about demons today?' I asked. A murmur of excitement rippled through the room.

'Demons *would* be more fun,' said Thom the manticore shifter from behind me.

'Yeah, can we learn about demons?' other students echoed.

'We're not scheduled to cover demons until next semester,' Dasko said tilting his head at me, 'but I guess they are pretty interesting.' I beamed at him and heard more excited mutters. With a wink, Dasko waved his hand and the lights dimmed.

'There are many types of creatures in Olympus. Even though monsters, demons and Gods are all different beings, they can all be monstrous, demonic and divine. It is important to remember that.' Dasko gave me a pointed look, and the flames in the iron dish leaped white. When they faded, there was a collective gasp from the class. My brain struggled to process the image of the creature shown in the dish. It was a fierce looking man, but from the waist down were two writhing serpent bodies instead of legs, and where his fingers should be were snarling and snapping dragon heads. Enormous leathery wings protruded from his back and fire burned in his evil looking eyes.

'This is Typhon, father of monsters. Born from the earth and Tartarus, the depths of hell itself,' Dasko said. Tartarus was where the Titans were imprisoned. I recoiled at the thought of being trapped in a place where something like this creature had been created. 'He mated with Echidna, a woman who was half snake and would become known as the mother of monsters. Many of her offspring still terrorize Olympus today, though the gods now keep a lot of them as pets.' A look of distaste flashed across Dasko's face. 'Monsters such as three-headed dogs, giant sea monsters, winged lions, monstrous eagles and vicious dragons.' Images of the creatures hovered in the dish, then vanished, replaced by the next.

'Then there are demigod demons, the offspring of gods that carry deadly tasks or tastes. There are gods of all that mortals fear, such as Thanatos the god of death,

Erebus the god of darkness and Phobetor the god of nightmares. And they all control their own demons. Like the Furies, demon goddesses of vengeance. And the Empusa, demigoddesses who live off warm human blood.' An image of a creepy veiled figure floated in the dish and my skin crawled. 'Or Eurynomos, demon of rotting corpses.' Thankfully, the image didn't change to show what he looked like. 'The demons of violent death, for example, are called Keres, and the demons of plague and sickness are the Nosoi.'

'Why are there no pictures of those?' asked Tak, a few seats down from me, when the image in the dish still hadn't changed.

'We don't know what some of them look like. If you come across a lot of these demons, you won't live to paint a picture,' Dasko said and fear gnawed at my insides, anxiety rippling through me. 'The point is, monsters are one thing, but demons are quite another. They usually have god-given duties to fulfill and they will stop at nothing to carry out their master's tasks. Many have ichor in their veins, like all of you, and some of the ancient ones have immense power.' The professor waved his hand and though the room was flooded with warm light again, the chill that had settled across my skin didn't lessen. 'Right. Whether or not that's satisfied your curiosity, we'll get back to Hera's family tree,' Dasko announced without looking at me. Everyone hurried to open their notebooks and the flame dish image changed to show Hera, regal and beautiful, but I barely registered her likeness.

What kind of demons had I let out of that box?

. . .

Over the next day, the thought of the monsters and demons Dasko had described consumed me. I ignored my friends' invitations to play games after dinner and instead buried myself amongst the bookshelves, hunting for books about the creatures who had shared the world of Olympus with Oceanus before he vanished. But I couldn't find anything useful. Icarus helped me search through volume after volume, as he was still much better at ancient language than I was, but all we could establish was that Oceanus had gone missing shortly after Prometheus had been mysteriously freed from the eagles that tortured him daily.

'So why did he trap the demons in the box? And why these three?' I sighed, leaning against the hard wood of the shelves.

'We don't know for sure that he did,' said Icarus. 'It could have been someone else who hid the box.'

I scowled at him.

'And hid it underwater? No, it was Oceanus.' I *knew* it was, somehow. 'And that pearl I found, in the attic. I'm sure we need it for something,' I added.

'Maybe Professor Fantasma will know something about the pearl. Take it to Advanced Magical Objects class and ask her,' he suggested.

'What if she gets suspicious?'

Icarus snorted.

'If it's an interesting magical object, she'll forgive you,' he muttered.

'You don't know that. She might take it to Hermes.'

We had yet to see our godly headmaster for the semester, save for a short glimpse of him the day our new lessons kicked off. Chiron was still at the academy, teaching archery, so in my head I still saw him as running the school.

'I doubt it. And Fantasma knows you're a Titan. She won't be that suspicious that you have a Titan relic.'

'Hmmm,' I said skeptically.

'I'm running out of suggestions,' Icarus said, looking at me. His green eyes shone and for the first time in days my head emptied of demons. For a blissful moment, there was just him and those mesmerizingly beautiful eyes.

A piercing scream ripped through my moment. We both whirled our heads towards the noise, then we were running between the bookshelves. We burst out into the common area to see a large group of people huddled around something on the floor. I hurried over, pushing through people and leaving Icarus and his big wings behind. When I got through the crowd I saw Zali, crouched down.

'What-' I started to ask her, then gasped and stumbled backward. A dryad girl I vaguely recognized from the year above us was sprawled out on the floor. Her normally tan skin was as white as the marble tiles beneath her and her open, staring eyes were completely black. Zali looked up at me, face panicked and pale.

'I don't think she's breathing,' she croaked.

'Get Fantasma!' I said, turning to the nearest student.

'Somebody's already gone for her,' the boy answered, his eyes fixed on the dryads motionless face. Her mouth was open in a silent scream. I shuddered and watched her chest, hoping to see it move. Nothing happened.

'Get out of the way,' a voice rasped, and cold rippled across my arm as Professor Fantasma swept past me, her ghostly form going straight through my elbow. She crouched as she reached the girl, touching her neck, then peering at her unmoving eyes.

'What happened?' she asked, the silent crowd holding their breath as they watched.

'She... floated in the air. She screamed, then fell,' stammered a tall, waif-like girl standing behind Zali. Her hands were shaking and she wouldn't look at the dryad girl's black eyes.

'I need someone to carry her,' Professor Fantasma said, standing up straight. I felt movement behind me, and turned to see the crowd part for Chiron.

'Lay her on my back,' he said gravely. Thom, Tak and two boys I didn't know rushed forwards and lifted her lifeless body from the ground, onto the centaurs back. Her limbs were awkward and clunky and I shuddered.

'Is she...' Zali didn't finish the whispered question, but everybody looked at Professor Fantasma for the answer.

'She's alive. But her soul is no longer in her body. Or in the academy.'

My stomach dropped at her words, fear crawling over my skin as my heart hammered. How could a person's soul be separated from their body?

'Everybody to their dorms, now!' bellowed Chiron. There was a scramble as panicked motion set in, students rushing to grab their stuff and make for the safety of their rooms. I stared after the dryad girl as Chiron strode carefully towards the front temple, jumping when Icarus laid his hand on my shoulder.

'We can't go to the tower tonight,' he said quietly. 'It might not be safe.'

'What if...' I looked up at him, the question pounding through my head, making me feel sick. 'What if it's one of the demons?' *What if I caused this?*

'We don't know what happened to her yet, Dora. It might be a dryad thing.'

'What, dryads often just lose their souls after dinner?' I didn't mean to speak so harshly, but my frayed nerves were fueling my emotions and I couldn't help it.

'Dora, come on, we need to go,' Zali appeared beside me, wide-eyed and holding out my backpack. I took it from her, mutely. 'Miss Alma is escorting students to the girls dorm now, we don't want to be left here.' The fear in her voice set my skin prickling again.

'I'll see you tomorrow,' Icarus said softly to me, and I stared into his eyes a second longer before Zali tugged me towards the temple doors.

4

I felt no sense of relief or safety when we got back to our room, only a quiet terror that I had caused something this terrible to happen. Zali told me the girl's name was Dimitra and as I lay in my bed that night, the image of her black, staring eyes filled my dreams.

'Attention students.' A loud voice dragged me from uneasy sleep.

'That's Hermes!' I heard Zali squeak from the other side of my curtain.

'Classes shall continue as normal today. Please report anything suspicious to your nearest teacher.' The voice echoed around the little dorm room. I waited for more, for reassurance that they had found the reason for Dimitra's collapse, that they had healed her, but there was nothing.

'Is that it?' I sat up in my bed, rubbing my tired eyes.

'I guess so,' said Zali, pulling back my curtain and

giving me a worried look. 'They wouldn't be sending us to class if it wasn't safe,' she said.

'I wouldn't be so sure,' I muttered, swinging my legs out of bed. 'Isn't the academy all about preparing us for the brutal world of Olympus?'

'Yeah but... her *soul* was gone,' Zali whispered, eyes wide and puffy. I realized as I looked at her that she hadn't gotten much sleep either.

'You're right,' I said, with a smile. 'They wouldn't risk our souls, I'm sure.'

I hoped the words were true.

There was a nervous buzz about the students in flying class, everyone whispering and muttering about Dimitra. My eavesdropping got me no new information - it sounded like nobody knew anything. My second class was fire element with Neos, and a pulsing nervousness was making my stomach feel jittery as we waited outside the elements building for the teacher.

'Did you do it, dirty Titan scum? Did you steal Dimitra's soul?' sneered Arketa, pushing through the crowd to stand in front of me.

I scowled at her.

'Back off, Arketa,' I said, turning away from her. I had more important things to worry about than her today.

'Hear that, everyone? She's not denying it.' My fists clenched by my sides and I turned back to her.

'I had nothing to do with it, and you know it,' I growled.

'It's exactly the kind of thing a monster like you would

do,' she said, venom in her voice. Anger pulsed through me, mingling with my frayed nerves.

'You seriously think I go about stealing souls?'

'Why not? It's what Titan's do. You're dangerous, you *and* your boyfriend,' she spat. 'You shouldn't be allowed in the school. Nothing like this happened before you came here.' A muttering started around her and I felt sick. The other students were listening to her. They believed her.

'What is your problem?' I shouted, the tired frustration getting the better of me. 'We're just normal students!' As I spoke, a flame burst from my hand, shooting towards Arketa. I stared in dumb horror as she screamed and a wall of water appeared from nowhere in front of her, catching the flame and instantly dousing it.

'Detention, Pandora,' said a smooth, deep voice. Everybody jumped and turned as Professor Neos spoke.

'But I didn't... That wasn't me! I can't even make flames like that! I-' He cut off my stammered protests.

'I saw it with my own eyes. Detention. This lunchtime, with me.' He stopped in front of me and my stomach lurched as he gave me a tiny smile and his beautiful brown eyes flashed scarlet red.

I kept my head down for the whole class, doing my very best to avoid eye contact with the striking teacher. Arketa avoided me like the plague, which I was fine with, practicing in the opposite corner of the room. When the gong rang and everyone began to file out of the room, Neos called,

'Stay here please, Pandora.' I gulped.

When everyone else had left the room I looked slowly at Neos. He grinned back at me.

'Pandora,' he said, eyes shining. 'I've been waiting for the right opportunity to speak to you. Alone.' My skin prickled.

'It wasn't me. That flame. I didn't do it,' I said.

He waved his hand dismissively.

'Oh, I know. I did.'

My mouth fell open.

'I needed an excuse to give you detention.'

'Why?' I whispered, but I already knew the answer. His eyes burned crimson as he stepped towards me.

'I wanted to say thank you, dear girl. You released me from that cursed box.'

I started to run before he finished speaking, but a gust of air coiled around me, tugging me backward, and a wall of fire burst from the ground, blocking the exit.

'Woah, woah, I'm not going to hurt you, little Titan. I want to help you!' The gust stopped and I staggered backward.

'Who are you?' I gasped, my heart pounding so hard I thought it would burst from my chest.

'Neos,' he shrugged. 'A lowly demon, trapped in that box with those two other fools for all the wrong reasons. But now I am free, thanks to you, and we can go and find Oceanus.'

'Why would you want to find him? Didn't he trap you?'

'Mistakenly, yes. But Titans and Olympians need to

roam this world together, and he and Prometheus can make that happen.'

The words of the poem rang in my mind.

'You want peace?' I asked warily. 'What kind of demon are you?'

'A fire demon,' he grinned, and a halo of flames appeared over his head, casting flickering orange shadows over his handsome face. 'Let me prove to you that I'm not a bad guy.'

I scowled at him.

'What happened to Dimitra?'

'The third demon. Soul snatcher,' he said distaste-fully. For a second I couldn't breathe. It *was* my fault.

'How... how do we get her soul back? How do we stop it?'

'The demon is one of the Keres. They're the demigod spirits of violent death. Normally they only take souls from the dying, but this one's gone rogue and has taken a soul from the living. They're not easy to catch though, and as for retrieving Dimitra's soul... Only an exception-ally powerful god could talk Hades into that. He owns the souls the Keres take.'

'A god like... like Oceanus,' I said slowly.

'Indeed,' he grinned at me. 'I'll tell you what. Let me teach you fire magic. Let me help you catch the death demon. Then, when you've seen I'm on your side, we can go and find Oceanus and return that student's soul.'

I regarded the demon, the fire halo still hovering above him. I believed that he didn't want to hurt me. After all, he'd had plenty of opportunity to do that already. And he was answering my questions. So far, this was the most information I'd managed to get about the box. And if he knew how to stop this Keres demon, then I really didn't have a choice.

'Alright then,' I said, warily and he clapped his hands together delightedly. 'How do we stop the death demon?'

'We'll need to lure it to us.'

'How?'

'You'll need to make a potion. It'll need ingredients. Very rare and dangerous ingredients.'

'I'm not studying potions until next semester,' I said.

'Then you're going to have to be a bit sneaky,' Neos said, red eyes flashing.

'Why can't you make it?' I asked.

'I'm a demon. If I touch powerful artifacts, boom.' His flame halo burst into a small explosion behind his head and I jumped back. 'Demons no-touchy,' he grinned.

I narrowed my eyes at him.

'How do I know I can trust you?' I said.

'You don't. But I know how to find Oceanus and nobody else does, so... the way I see it you don't really have a choice if you want to stop the soul snatcher.'

I rolled my eyes.

'That's blackmail.'

He shrugged.

'I *am* a demon. It's how I operate.' He gave me a cocky look. 'How about you let me give you some tips on fire magic, and then you decide?'

Before I could answer, flames leaped up around us in a burning hot ring and his eyes seemed to come alive. Fear shot through me, and I felt the presence of the ocean deep inside me. My power focused in on the water wall at the back of the room.

'Ignore the water, Pandora. Feel the fire,' Neos said quietly. 'Let the heat seep into your skin. Let the feeling burn through your veins, pump your heart, fill your chest. Let the heat in.'

His voice was seductive, impossible to resist, and I found myself doing what he instructed. Heat seared through me, not burning me but making me feel alive. I held my hands out as the power blazed through my limbs, and the ring around us roared into an inferno.

Neos cried out in delight and threw his own arms out. The flames disappeared in an instant. I gaped around me, my skin tingling and prickling, the oceans presence reassuringly back in place in my mind.

'Was that me?' I whispered.

'It sure was. I knew you had it in you,' he beamed.

'I... I don't want power like that,' I stammered, remembering the girl who had nearly burned down the school. 'I can't control the water, let alone...' I trailed off, picturing the roaring flames.

'You won't be able to do that again without me, don't worry. We'll work on it,' Neos said. I looked at him, surprised that I felt reassured by his words. His red eyes faded slowly back to brown as he looked back at me. 'We'll make a great team, Pandora,' he said.

5

'Y ou've got to be joking.' Icarus stared at me. 'You just had a private lesson in fire magic from a demon? What part of *be careful* did you not understand!'

'It's not my fault!' I protested. 'And if he knows how to stop the soul snatcher then we have to try.'

We were at our usual meeting place, at the top of the pegasus tower, but since I told Icarus what had happened in my detention with Neos, I suspected there wouldn't be any kissing tonight.

'Dora, the poem said we had to *kill* all the demons, not befriend them!'

'I haven't befriended him,' I rolled my eyes. 'I'm not stupid enough to trust him. But he knows things Icarus. We need him.'

Icarus rolled his eyes and turned away from me.

'Do you have any better suggestions?' I asked.

'No,' he answered eventually. 'But I don't like this.'

'Neither do I,' I said, laying a hand on his arm. 'But we

need to do what we can. It's better than sitting around helplessly.'

He looked at me, his eyes softening.

'It's not your fault, you know. What happened to Dimitra.'

'Of course it is,' I said, dropping my gaze. 'I let the demon loose.'

'But *you* didn't attack her. You don't need to risk your life to save hers.'

'Yes, Icarus. I do. I'm responsible and she's completely innocent.'

He fell silent.

'What if this potion Neos wants you to make is actually to make him stronger or something? What if it's not to lure the soul snatcher at all?' he asked suddenly.

'I thought that too,' I said. 'Once he's told me the ingredients, I'll ask Nix about them. He should know about that sort of stuff.'

Icarus nodded.

'OK then. Let's catch a Keres.'

'You're going to help?' Hope and gratitude filled me as I looked at him. He took my hand and squeezed it hard.

'Of course I am. I'll always help you, Dora.' His intense green eyes looked deep into mine and my breath caught.

Maybe there *would* be some kissing tonight after all.

It was Saturday the next day, and when I woke up I found a note had been left for me. I evaded Zali's curious questions with some made up nonsense about Icarus leaving

me a love letter, and she gave me a cute grin and left me
to open it in peace. I immediately felt bad for lying to her.

Pandora,

*The Keres are drawn to violent death. So assuming you don't want to kill
anybody, we will need the following ingredients to make the potion we discussed.*

Fire rafe

Human blood

Manticore feather

Rust from the armor of a hero who died in battle

Good luck! Neos

I blew out a long breath. Well I was human, so the blood
was easy enough, as long as we only needed a little bit. A
manticore feather... I had no idea where to start. I also
had no idea what a fire rafe was, and as for rust from the
armor of a hero who died in battle... My mind flashed on
the Magical Objects classroom, filled with ancient relics.
Surely there was something in there?

For our weekend chores we cleaned the showers
together with two girls from the next dorm room, and as
usual they gave me a wide berth. I listened in on their
conversation though, which was dominated by chat
about Dimitra. The dryad girl had been moved to the
guest rooms in the front temple, one of the girls had
heard, and there had been no change in her condition. I
scrubbed at the bathroom tiles harder, resolving to go to

the magical objects classroom that afternoon, to talk to Nix and to look for rusty armor. I needed to help her as soon as I could. But when we returned to our rooms we found a note pinned to every door announcing an impromptu archery tournament that afternoon.

'I wonder if that's so that they can keep an eye on us all together?' said Zali. That made sense, I thought, but it would make carrying out my new plan impossible that afternoon.

We met Tak and Icarus down by the training field. An unavoidable thrill rippled through me when I spotted his massive black wings in the crowd. They were magnificent.

'So, archery time,' grinned Tak, rubbing his hands together as we reached him.

'Reckon you're going to win this time?' Zali teased him.

'For sure,' he answered, jutting his chin out.

'Nope. I'm going to beat you today,' I told him with a wicked smile.

He'd come tenth last time. I had come twelfth. There were just under eighty students in the school, so we were both pretty good, but our months training in swords and spears together was making us more and more competitive with each other.

'You're on, Titan girl,' he said, wiggling his eyebrows at me. Icarus laughed.

'Please beat him, Dora,' he said. 'We won't be able to bear the smugness if he wins.' Icarus's laugh was cut off when Agrius stamped through the middle of our group. Tak started to protest but fell quiet when he realized who it was pushing past us. Chiron trotted in his wake, smiling kindly at the students around him.

'Everyone ready?' Agrius boomed as he got to the middle of the training field. We all cheered in agreement. 'Five groups. Knockout rounds,' he yelled and the air fizzed with electricity, then colored sashes appeared around all our shoulders. The four of us all had different colors and I was wearing red. That meant I would compete with the other reds and the top two of us would go on to compete with the top two of the other groups.

'Good luck,' I said, and headed off to where the red sashes were gathering. Zali jogged off to the blues, Tak sauntered to the greens and Icarus skulked towards the yellows.

My group was a mix of students from each year, and thankfully none of Arketa's crowd were wearing a red sash. Vronti was though.

'I heard you got detention,' he said to me as I reached the group. I paused in surprise. The silver-haired Zeus twin had never spoken a word to me before.

'Uh, yeah,' I muttered.

'As head of year, I need to reprimand you,' he sneered and defensiveness pricked at me.

'Reprimand me? Wasn't that what the detention was for?'

'You're setting a bad example. You attacked a student.'

'No I didn't!'

'There were ten eye-witnesses,' he said, folding his slender arms.

I clenched my hands into fists at my side and gritted

my teeth. He was never going to believe that Neos had created the flame.

'Fine,' I hissed.

'Dusting library bookshelves. An hour every night next week,' he said, and turned away from me.

'What! But I-'

He whirled back to me, cutting off my protest.

'Want to make it two weeks, Titan girl?' he snarled, his grey eyes boring into mine. I closed my mouth and glared at him. 'I thought not.' He gave me a smug smile and joined the line of students waiting their turn to shoot at the targets. I seethed at his back, the anger making me hyper-aware of the churning currents around the school. Why was he allowed to hand out double punishments? I had too much to do trying to save Dimitra's soul to be dusting bookshelves! Guilt that it was my fault Dimitra's soul needed saving in the first place crept through the anger. I would just have to manage, I told myself.

By the time it was my turn to shoot a grim resolution had settled where the playful competitiveness had been. I would show Vronti that I wasn't weak or soft. I picked up a bow from the stack beside me and nocked an arrow. Drawing back the string as far as I could, I released a long breath out, focused on the red circle in the center of the target twenty feet away and loosed. It thudded into the target, dead center. Nobody clapped. I was the Titan girl, they weren't going to cheer for me. I nocked a second arrow quickly, and aimed at the next target, twenty-five feet away. My arrow landed just outside the red center circle. The third target, thirty feet away, was always the hardest to get right, but I landed my last arrow easily inside the second ring.

Satisfaction thrummed through me as Agrius peered at my arrows, then nodded reluctantly.

'Vronti and Pandora. Next round.' The other students trudged away to sit in the temporary bleachers now lining the back of the field. Tak waved at me as I approached him, standing with another boy in a green sash.

'Nice shooting,' he said.

'Vronti gave me an hours worth of chores every night next week,' I growled.

'That sucks,' Tak frowned.

'Tell me about it.'

'So now you need to beat him at archery? I like the motivation,' he grinned. 'But I'm still gonna win.'

'Huh,' I grunted. Currents surged through the ocean around us, and I glanced up at the dome. Power pulsed through the water, massive and strong and lethal and I felt it in my veins. I could beat Tak *and* Vronti.

I was matched with the winner of the yellow group, and easily landed my arrows inside the smallest two rings, moving me through to the next round. I felt my focus tightening as the competition progressed, steady energy pumping through me and making me more determined. In no time at all there were only four of us left. Vronti, Tak and an eagle-shifter girl called Alexsis. Her eyesight was excellent, and I knew she would be tough to beat. But as long as I came out ahead of the two boys, I'd be happy.

Tak went first. He got his first arrow in the red center circle easily. But his next two went wide, and he only just made the thirty feet target. He gave me a shrug as he walked past me standing in line.

'I might still beat you,' he said cheerfully.

Vronti went next. His first two arrows made the red circle, and his third landed on the outer edge of the smallest ring. It was a good effort, but I'd already managed similar. Adrenaline started to flow through me as I stepped up to take my go. I could beat him.

My first arrow hit dead center on the closest target. I moved onto the second quickly, sharpening my focus on the middle of the target. On a long breath out, I loosed. My arrow flew straight into the middle of the red dot. Satisfaction coursed through me and I did a little fist pump. One more to go. My hands stayed steady as I aimed, and I knew when I loosed it was a good shot. It landed almost exactly where Vronti's arrow had, but it was too far away to see which was closer. I heard a collective intake of breath from the spectators as Agrius stomped over to the target and peered at it. After a long moment, where I almost forgot to breathe, the big man reluctantly pointed at me. Vronti glared at me, then strode away towards the bleachers. A ripple of clapping sounded and I turned to see Tak, Zali, Icarus and Gida cheering for me. Warmth flooded my chest.

'Very nice,' said Alexsis, walking past me. 'But you're not going to win.' The smile she gave me was a friendly one though, and I realized her words were competitive rather than mean. It wouldn't be so bad if she won. After all, I'd beaten that silver-haired jerk and that's what mattered. I watched as she lifted the bow, drew back her elbow and took a deep breath. Then she froze, and I was close enough to see that her whole body was shaking. I stepped forwards, unsure what was happening, when suddenly she lifted off the ground, her head tipping backward and the bow clattering to the ground. I rushed forwards, just in time to catch her as she dropped, lifeless to the ground. We both tumbled to the floor, but I was able to keep her head from hitting the ground, catching her shoulders with my arm.

'Alexsis!' I shouted, lowering her gently to the grass and pushing her blonde hair back from her face. I gasped. Her eyes were solid, onyx back.

6

Everything after that was a bit of a blur. Chiron galloped over to me and Alexsis, and Agrius pushed me out of the way, easily lifting the girl onto his back. Miss Alma and Professor Fantasma appeared quickly, and began escorting panicked students to the dorms. I got to my feet slowly, relief washing over me when I saw Icarus hovering behind the centaur headmaster.

'Pandora, you were closest, did you see what happened?' Chiron asked me.

I shook my head mutely.

'She probably did it,' muttered Agrius loudly. Chiron glared at him. In a way though, Agrius was right. It was my fault.

'She froze, began shaking, then fell,' I whispered.

'Go back to your dorm now,' Chiron said gently. I nodded and walked past him and Icarus rushed over, wrapping his arms tight around me, his wings folding protectively around my body.

'Dora, that could have been you,' he breathed. I looked up at him. I hadn't even considered that. 'You went right before her...' He stared into my eyes, his concern and relief etched on his face.

'It should have been me,' I mumbled.

'No. No, only we can fix this, Dora. You need to stay safe.'

'I'm OK, Icarus,' I said. 'But we need to go to the Magical Objects classroom.'

He looked at me and I could tell he was about to say we shouldn't so I spoke before he could.

'We have to try and do *something*. Like you just said, we're the only ones who can.'

'Pandora, Icarus, to your rooms, now!' yelled Miss Alma, her voice penetrating the bubble Icarus had cocooned us in with his wings. He leaned forwards, kissing me quickly on the cheek.

'I'll meet you there at ten tonight,' he whispered.

'Thank you,' I whispered back gratefully. Then he was gone, jogging towards the boys dorms. I turned in the opposite direction, picking up my pace when I saw Zali.

'Are you alright?' I asked as I caught up to her just outside the girls dorm building.

'Oh, Dora!' she cried, and threw her arms around me as she burst into tears.

She was still sniffing half an hour later, when we were huddled together on her bed, wrapped in blankets.

'It could have been you or Tak,' she said for the tenth time.

'But it wasn't. We're both fine,' I said as reassuringly as I could, stroking her arm.

'But what if you'd gone in a different order? What if-'

I cut her off.

'Zali,' I said sternly. 'We're both fine. And Alexsis and Dimitra are both alive. There's every chance they'll both be fine too. Everything is OK.' I desperately wanted to believe what I was telling her. Her big, red-rimmed amber eyes looked into mine.

'You're right,' she said with a small smile. 'I'm sorry. I just care about you both so much.'

I squeezed her hand.

'I know you do. Particularly Tak...' I said, with a sideways look and an eyebrow wiggle.

She blushed and dropped her gaze.

'Oh, Dora. I'm only admitting this because I'm over-emotional but... yeah. Particularly Tak. When I think about him with those horrible black eyes...' She shuddered and I squeezed her hand tight.

'How long have you liked him?' I asked her.

'Forever. Like honestly, from the first time I saw him at the academy. Then when he stood up to Filis for me... I've not been able to think about anybody else since.'

'Why don't you tell him?' I asked her.

She frowned at me.

'He doesn't like me back. He likes Roz.' She pulled a face.

'You don't know that!' I exclaimed. 'How would you know unless you ask him?'

She shook her head emphatically.

'No. He's my best friend. What if it ruined everything?'

I bit my lip, thinking. She had a point. But surely Tak fancied her? I mean, she was kind and funny and smart, not to mention gorgeous. And they got on great.

'Maybe you could try dropping some hints?' I suggested.

'Like what?'

'Um, ask him if he's into anybody at the moment. Tell him you're waiting for somebody you know you can be friends with. That kind of thing.'

'Oh, I don't know,' Zali said, looking worried. 'What if he's not interested?'

'Then at least you know, and you can turn your attention to a different sexy demigod,' I grinned.

'There are a few in this school,' she smiled back.

'There really are,' I agreed.

'And Professor Dasko...' We both fell silent, a dreamy look on Zali's face. 'Professor Neos is hot too,' she added, eventually. The demons red eyes flashed in my mind and I shifted uncomfortably.

'Yeah,' I muttered.

'Well, I guess you only have eyes for Icarus now,' Zali cooed. 'You two are so cute.'

'I wouldn't describe Icarus as cute,' I snorted.

'You're cute *together*.'

'If you say so,' I said with a smile.

We chatted a while longer, about boyfriends we'd had before coming to Olympus Academy, and before long Zali's eyes were completely dry and she was yawning.

'Time for bed,' she said, and shuffled down under her

blankets. 'Thanks, Dora. I'm going to think about what to say to Tak,' she said as I stood up from the bed.

'Good. Sleep well,' I said.

At ten on the dot, I was hovering in the shadows outside the Magical Objects classroom. I pressed myself against the building as I saw movement in the dim blue light, stepping forward again in relief when I recognized Icarus, his wings folded tight against his back. We didn't speak as he reached me, just turned and hurried down to the classroom. I expected it to be locked but the handle turned and the door swung open. We crept in and closed it behind us. The room was instantly dark, now that no light was filtering down from the dome into the underground room any more. I summoned a small, shaky fireball and it cast flickering shadows across Icarus's serious face.

'Find a lamp,' I whispered. 'I can't keep this up long and I don't want to set fire to anything in here. Nix would not be pleased if we burned his feather,' I muttered as Icarus hurried over to the big table in the middle of the room and began looking around for an oil lamp. He found one, and once it was lit, purple tinted light shone brightly around the room, illuminating the shelves of items clearly. I made my way to where Nix's cushion lived.

'Isn't it a bit late for you to be in here?' was the first thing the phoenix said to me.

'Hello Nix,' I said. 'It's sort of an emergency.'

'*I'm sure,*' he drawled. '*This had better not be boy trouble.*'

'It's not! I found out what the third demon is.'

'*What? How?*'

I paused and I heard him groan mentally.

'*You spoke to the red demon, didn't you?*'

'He spoke to me! But yeah. He says he's a fire demon, trapped by Oceanus by mistake, and he wants to help us unite Titans and Olympians,' I summarized quickly.

'*A fire demon? There's no such thing,*' replied Nix.

'Really?' I said surprised. 'Well, that's what he said. And he's really good with fire. He also said that the third demon is a Keres demon.'

The phoenix drew in a sharp breath, the sound clear in my head.

'*You'd know about it if you had one of those loose in the academy. Students would be dying.*'

I said nothing, the sick feeling in my stomach returning.

'*Pandora...*' Nix said slowly. '*Please tell me people aren't dying.*'

'No. They're not dying. But, um, there are two students missing their souls.'

'*Great Zeus, this is bad,*' the bird cursed. '*You need to stop that demon. But it won't be easy. And the souls will be lost to Hades forever.*'

'What? No! Neos said we can get the souls back, if we find Oceanus!'

'*Oceanus? He knows where he is?*' Excitement tinged the birds voice.

'He claims he knows how to find him, yes. He gave me

the ingredients to make a potion that would lure the death demon to us. He says that once he's proven he can be trusted, he'll tell me how to get to Oceanus.'

'*What were the ingredients?*' Nix asked. I told him quickly. '*That's a potion of battle doom. It would draw a Keres demon to you sure enough,*' he muttered. Relief washed through me.

'Is it true that Oceanus can get the stolen souls back from Hades?'

'*Oceanus is one of the most powerful ancient gods of all time. If anyone can, he can,*' said Nix. '*He could also restore me to a new phoenix body.*'

'What? Really?' Excitement pulsed through me. 'That would be amazing!'

'*Hmm,*' grunted the bird. '*It's not easy to get the attention of a Titan though.*'

'If he's trapped and I free him then he'll owe me a favor! I promise I'll ask him,' I told Nix.

'*Let's not get ahead of ourselves,*' he muttered, but I was sure his voice had softened.

'What's a fire rafe?' I asked him.

'*A very toxic plant that grows in underwater volcanoes. You won't find any in the academy.*' My heart sank. '*But... I remember you telling me about that highly cultivated aqua garden underneath the school...*'

'Yes! There are all sorts of plants where the cave was!'

'*Then look there. You'll find a picture of it in any books about plants from Hephaestus's realm, Scorpio.*'

'OK, thanks.'

'*And as for the armor rust, that will be kept somewhere in the school. It's a very powerful, very dark ingredient. It'll be locked up somewhere safe.'*

'Somewhere like the advanced tower?'

'I imagine so, yes.'

'Right. I'll get on it,' I said, standing up.

'Keep me informed,' Nix answered, a departure from his usually more grumpy goodbye.

'Will do. Bye Nix,' I said, and placed the feather back on its cushion.

I relayed the conversation back to Icarus, who looked slightly less worried than he had before.

'I guess if Nix says it sounds alright then it must be. He has no reason to lie to you.'

'Exactly,' I answered. 'Now, do we sneak out into the ocean to look for the plant, or break into the advanced tower first?'

7

When Zali and I went down to breakfast the next morning the mood was quiet and tense, everybody chatting in hushed whispers again. It was as though nobody wanted to draw attention to themselves.

'Morning,' Tak said as we sat down opposite him. There was no sign of Icarus yet.

'Is there any news about Alexsis?' Gida asked, quickly.

'Nothing from the girls dorms,' Zali told him. He blew out a sigh.

'Were you friends?' I asked him.

'Yeah. She's been here a few years.'

'I'm sorry,' I said, after a pause.

'Not your fault,' the satyr said, looking glumly at his bowl of porridge. Guilt clenched at my stomach, my appetite vanishing.

. . .

'Ah, Pandora,' said a voice behind me. I turned to see Dasko standing there, arms bulging as he folded them. 'Eat up, you've got extra lessons today.'

'What?' I stared at him. Extra lessons? It was Sunday.

'Yep. I've got an idea about how we can harness some of your water power. I'm fed up of getting wet in class,' he said with a smirk.

'But, I have stuff I need to do today!' I protested. The professor frowned at me.

'Pandora, there is nothing you need to do more than get control of your power,' he said, his voice low and serious. I looked nervously around at the other students, looking over curiously. I did *not* need them to think I was in danger of losing control.

'Right. Sure,' I said quickly.

'Good. Meet me at the pool in half an hour.'

'Gods, you're so lucky!' grinned Zali after he'd gone.

I groaned.

'How do you figure that? I've got detention every day next week and now I have to spend Sunday in extra classes!'

'Extra classes with *Dasko*! In the pool...' She raised her eyebrows at me and I rolled my eyes.

'Why does everyone fancy him?' grumbled Tak, covering his porridge in sugar. 'He's just a normal guy.'

I hung on to Tak's words as I reached the pool a half hour later. Dasko was already in the water, shirtless and he really didn't look like a normal guy to me. His back and arms bulged with muscles as he powered through the water in laps. I concentrated on the thought of Icarus. I thought about his beautifully intense green eyes and the feel of his stunning wings wrapped around me and all at once, I felt less intimidated by the gorgeous professor.

I slipped into the pool, the power of the water humming around me. When Dasko reached the pool edge he stood, pushing his wet hair from his face.

'Ah,' he said, when he saw me. 'So, I thought we'd try something. Instead of trying to work with less water, maybe we should be trying with more. After all, what you did with that sea demon last semester was incredible.'

'I had Icarus though,' I told him. 'We worked together.'

'True,' the teacher nodded, 'but you were able to control the water.'

I thought about that.

'There was a pretty strong motivation,' I said, eventually.

'Then give yourself a strong motivation now. What drives you, Pandora?'

'Catching the demons and saving the stolen souls,' I said, immediately.

Dasko frowned at me.

'Half of what you're saying I can understand. You want to catch the demons. But the second thing you're saying in that Titan language that I can't understand... Have you found something out?'

I nodded. Excitement filled his eyes.

'That's great! Now, take that drive, that *need* and make sure you use it. Remind yourself why you need to be able to control your power.'

'OK,' I said.

'Move the water from this end of the pool to the other,' Dasko instructed.

I merged my mind with the water, forcing it to flow away from us. It moved quickly, splashing up and over the edges of the pool.

'Now hold it there,' he said. I held the water still, but the longer I concentrated on being connected to it, the more its great, throbbing power grew in my mind. It roared and crashed and swelled and I couldn't contain it.

'Remember why you're doing this!' Dasko called as the shuddering mass of liquid teetered at the other end of the pool. Black onyx eyes filled my head. Wraith-like demons made of black smoke swirled around me, the crimson face leaping out at me. I had to be stronger to defeat them. I *needed* my power. Resolve tightened my grip on the churning power and the hovering water at the other end of the pool stilled.

'That's great! You can let it go now, but gently,' said Dasko. I lessened my grip as slowly as I could, but then I lost it completely and the water crashed back down into the pool, splashing over both of us.

'That was really good, Pandora,' Dasko beamed at me, water dripping from his hair. 'Now do it again.'

We practiced for hours, and it left me exhausted, but there was no doubt I was making progress. By the time I trudged up to my dorm to get washed up for dinner I was confident that I could hold all the water in the pool in place for a full five minutes. We had skipped lunch and I wolfed down a plate of pasta within minutes of plopping down next to my friends at the table.

'Wow,' said Tak, levitating a bowl of grated cheese towards himself. 'You're hungry.'

'Uhuh,' I grunted, still eating.

'I can't believe Dasko didn't let you stop for lunch,' grumbled Icarus beside me.

I swallowed my mouthful.

'We were making good progress. Neither of us wanted to stop,' I said.

Tiredness overwhelmed me almost as soon as the tables disappeared and the library shimmered into existence.

'I looked through the Scorpio books today,' Icarus said quietly to me as we made our way to our usual couch. 'I couldn't see any reference to a fire rafe.'

'Oh. That's disappointing,' I said, on a yawn. 'I'll look some more tomorrow during my shelf-dusting detention,' I scowled. 'Right now though, I'm going to bed.'

'OK. Well, good night.' His intense eyes were full of concern and I gave him a smile.

'Good night' I said, and stood on my tiptoes to kiss his cheek. His wings rustled and he gave me a flicker of a smile.

I slept badly. Swirling black smoke and gleaming red eyes haunted my dreams and I woke every few hours drenched in cold sweat, unable to shift the image of my friends lifeless and still with solid black irises.

I was still yawning when I filed into the hauler with Icarus and Zali for flying class after breakfast. I was hoping that the crisp ocean air would wake me up, and I inhaled deeply when we reached the top of the tower, as I always did.

'We have an obstacle course today, class!' called Miss Alma. 'Please saddle your steeds quickly and line up facing the first ring.' We followed her pointing arm to where six big rings were hanging, suspended in the air over the frothing sea. I jogged to Peto's stable right around the other side of the tower and he whinnied happily when he saw me.

'Hey, boy,' I said, and dragged the box over next to him to get him ready. He tucked his wings in to make it easier for me and a few minutes later we were lined up with nine other students. Icarus didn't have a Pegasus. He stood on the edge of the platform, rocking on his heels, wings twitching and expanded behind him. I could almost feel how much he wanted to jump from the ledge.

'I want you to fly through all six rings, lap the tower, then return here.' Miss Alma peered at us all to make sure we'd understood, then snapped her fingers. All of the floating rings roared to life with flickering flames. I let out a little gasp, adrenaline starting to surge through me. I reached out for the power of the sea below me, and drew it into myself. Peto and I could win this. Icarus glanced up at me, a wicked glint in his eye. He wanted to win too. I leaned forwards in my saddle.

'Go!' shouted Miss Alma. Peto raced to the edge and leaped. That brief moment of weightlessness took my breath away, as it always did, then I heard the pegasus's wings snapping taught and we were soaring towards the first ring. Peto had clearly done this before, because I barely needed to direct him. His head was jutted forwards, his wings beating hard as we closed in on the burning hoop. But Icarus was already there, his black wings gleaming with blue as he shot through the center of the first ring. Then I felt a jolt and we lurched to the side, towards the flames. Peto neighed as I realized what had happened. Kiko had deliberately crashed into us, and was now soaring easily through the hoop. I pulled on Peto's reigns and we turned sharply just in time, staying inside the burning ring. I narrowed my eyes and raced after the laughing blonde girl. She made it through the next two rings before me, Icarus still out in front, but there was a long gap between the third and fourth ring and I knew I could catch her. I spurred Peto on, shouting encouragements and we picked up speed. My hair whipped around my face as we dove towards the fourth ring, lower than the others. Kiko's laugh cut off abruptly as we sailed past her, flying through the fiery ring ahead of her.

'Yeah!' I cheered, hearing Peto whinny back. Now to catch Icarus. An ear splitting screech cut through my little celebration. I jerked my head around towards the noise and stared wide-eyed. Kiko was hovering above her Pegasus, body shaking and head thrown back. Horror filled me as I realized what was about to happen next.

'Peto, come on!' I urged the pegasus around and raced towards Kiko, as her limp body began to fall through the sky. But she was falling too fast. A black streak beneath me caught my eye and I realized with a bolt of hope that it was Icarus. He crashed into Kiko, and my heart almost stopped beating as they tumbled through the sky together. I thought desperately about how I could use the water to break their fall but if Kiko was unconscious she would drown. Then Icarus's wings spread wide, and he was moving up again, Kiko limp in his arms. Eight other pegasus and their riders galloped through the air, the first rider to reach him helping to lay her body across the white pegasus's back.

Miss Alma was tight-lipped and wide-eyed when we got back to the tower.

'Give her space! And someone get Fantasma and Agrius,' she said, as we crowded around Kiko. I didn't need to look at her to know her eyes were solid black. Nausea surged inside me.

'Are you alright?' gasped Icarus, stepping up beside me and Peto.

'Yes, of course,' I said, focusing on him. 'Icarus you were amazing. You saved her life.'

He said nothing, breathing heavily and leaning his hands on his knees.

'I didn't know you could fly that fast.'

'Nor did I. Guess it's all about motivation,' he muttered through panted breaths. That's what Dasko had said in the pool, I realized.

'We have to get into the advanced tower as soon as

possible,' I said quietly. 'And find out more about the fire rafe.'

Icarus nodded at me.

'We'll go tonight.'

8

When the hauler reached the bottom of the tower Hermes's voice rang out across the school and the feverish, scared hum of voices around me fell silent immediately.

'All students to the main temple. Now.'

I looked at Icarus and he reached for my hand as we followed the group towards the main temple. It was lined with bench seats, like it had been for the end of semester ceremony, and we all filed in to sit down. I looked around for Zali and eventually spotted her with Tak, Gida and Roz, three rows in front of us.

'Icarus,' a female voice said. We both turned and saw Arketa behind us, eyes rimmed with red. 'They told me what you did,' she said quietly. 'Thank you.'

'Um, yeah, sure,' he answered her awkwardly.

'It'll be OK, Arketa,' I told her, as reassuringly as I could manage.

'Don't even speak to me, witch,' she hissed, her eyes filling with tears and pure hatred as she glared at me. I took an involuntary step backward, her viciousness shocking me. 'I heard *everything* that happened up there. Alexsis was going to beat you at archery and Kiko was going to beat you at flying and now look at them both.' A tear spilled down her cheek.

'No, no, Arketa, I...' I wanted to tell her it wasn't me, but I knew, deep-down that really it was. It *was* my fault.

'Icarus, if you know what's good for you, you'll stay away from her. She's dangerous.' More tears spilled from her eyes and she turned and stamped past the other students behind us. Guilt and fear wrenched at my stomach.

'Nobody believes you're doing it, Dora. Don't worry,' said Icarus, squeezing my hand.

'But... what if I *am* dangerous?' I whispered. Icarus looked around pointedly at the students surrounding us.

'You're not. We'll talk later.'

I said nothing as we sat down, and within a minute Hermes was striding out onto the stage. In the presence of an Olympian, it was impossible to focus on anything else. The red-haired man had an almost visible glow around him, and it was as though the room was suddenly too small. He was wearing an ancient style toga and tiny shining gold wings fluttered at his ankles.

'A rogue death demon appears to be loose in the academy.' Gasps filled the hall at the god's blunt words. 'Athena and I have petitioned Zeus, but he insists that we do not intervene. He believes it is a prime test of the school's ability.' I gaped at Icarus as outraged and appalled shouts echoed through the room. Hermes held up his hand and the students fell quiet instantly. 'I do not agree with Zeus's decision, but I can't change it,' he said gravely. 'I will help wherever I can. All students will now be armed at all times. Your classes will be altered slightly to teach you more about demons and fighting, particularly the younger students. Potions that ward off spirits will be served at breakfast - make sure that you drink them.' Hermes ran a hand through his beard and looked around at us all. 'This academy is not popular with all of the gods. Let us prove that we are worthy. Kill the demon. Show Zeus what you can do.' Renewed mutters, lively and hopeful, rippled across the temple. 'And don't forget to drink the breakfast potions.' There was a flash of white light, and the god vanished. The mutters erupted into loud chatter and I listened speechless to the students around me.

'Hermes wants *us* to kill the demon?'

'If the potions work then we don't need to worry about anyone else being taken!'

'Does that mean we're all safe again now?'

'How do you kill a demon?'

'I can't wait for the new classes, demons aren't supposed to be until second year!'

'I wonder what weapons we'll get?'

I looked at Icarus, still gripping my hand.

'This is really good, Dora. Potions to keep us all safe,' he said, with a smile.

'Yes,' I nodded.

'Do you think we still need to make the luring potion?'

'If Neos says that's the best way to lure the demon then... yeah. I guess so.'

'Your attention please!' We all looked up at Chiron, now standing where Hermes had been. The centaur looked tight-lipped and angry. 'On your way out of the temple, please collect a potion and weapon from Agrius and Miss Alma. Then make your way to your next class as usual.' Everyone stood up at once, eager to get their hands on things that would make them safe. 'And please remember, all the teachers here can help you. If you are in trouble, or see anything suspicious, come and find us.' Chiron's eyes were beseeching, but most of the students ignored him, pushing their way towards Miss Alma and Agrius at the exit.

The potion Miss Alma gave me was bitter and sharp, but there wasn't much of it in the little glass vial so I gulped it down in one. I tucked the tiny, glinting dagger I'd chosen from selection of knives and slingshots into the side of my backpack. I couldn't see how a dagger would help fight an invisible demon that snatched souls. Hopefully the safety potion would leave the knife redundant. At lunchtime though, everyone was comparing weapons and talking animatedly about how they would catch and kill the demon.

'I mean, the problem is finding it, isn't it,' Tak said.

'Um, I don't think that's the only problem,' frowned Zali. 'What would you do with it once you found it?'

'Stab it, obviously,' he replied, levitating his dagger off the table and waving it in front of her. She rolled her eyes, but she was smiling. The tense fear from the last few days had lifted, and the confidence of the safety potion and the challenge set for the school was buoying everybody's spirits. I knew I should feel pleased that the secret was out, that Icarus and I were no longer carrying the burden alone, but instead I only felt a sick, hollow feeling in my stomach. Kiko, Alexsis, Dimitra... They were all lying lifeless in the front temple, their souls stolen. And now everybody was acting like killing the demon was a game. When I wasn't thinking about the soul snatcher, Arketa's hatred dominated my thoughts. She truly hated me. Why?

I kept my head down in fire class, practicing making little fireballs at the back of the room. I considered trying what Neos had shown me, letting the heat meld with my skin and flow through me, but I resisted the temptation. I didn't want to lose control of fire in a room full of students.

'Pandora, I heard the head boy gave you extended detentions after your attack on that poor girl last week,' said Neos, coming over to me.

I glared at him.

'That's right,' I said, through gritted teeth.

'Well, I've spoken to him, and your detentions will be spent with me instead.'

'What?'

'You could do with the practice,' he said, raising his

eyebrows at my little fireball. It disintegrated under his withering look. 'Fire classroom, after dinner. Every night this week.' The red flashed in his eyes for a split-second before he strolled away again.

When I told Icarus at dinner that night, his green eyes were dark and angry.

'I don't like this, Dora. I don't trust him,' he ground out.

'Nor do I. But there's nothing I can do about it. We need him. Plus he's a professor. I can't say no to detention.'

After dinner I left Icarus looking for more books about Scorpio in the library and stomped back to the fire classroom. Neos was leaning casually against a column outside the five elemental doors.

'Pandora,' he said as I approached. I scowled at him.

'This is stupid. I have to go and get the stuff you told me to find, and save the souls that have been taken,' I snapped at him.

'There's no hurry, little Titan. You've all got your magic potions to protect you from her now, and those souls aren't going anywhere,' he smiled. I knew I should feel annoyed at him calling me little Titan, but part of me kind of liked it. It was better than 'Titan scum'.

'Whatever,' I grumbled.

'Tell me, Pandora. Which of these doors are you most drawn to?'

I started to answer straight away but he held his hand up.

'Wait. Feel it. Try to really feel it. Which door is the strongest?'

I sighed, and stared at each door in turn. The air door, with the white gust carefully carved on it, felt cool and distant and out of reach. The electricity door, with its massive yellow lightning bolt, felt like nothing at all. It was just stone to me as I stared. The earth door, the elaborate root pattern leading up to a tree decorating it, gave me a slightly warm buzz when I focused on it, but little more. The water door though... Heaving, swelling, barely contained energy thrummed from the stone, the ground, the dome above me, filling my muscles with strength. I opened my mouth to speak but Neos cut me off again.

'Nuhuh, you have one more door,' he said, quietly. I looked at the fire door, concentrating. Heat, real and sharp and searing shot through my body, from head to foot. My skin tingled and fizzed and an elation began to take over my mind. It wasn't a feeling of strong, solid life-giving freedom like the water gave me. It was less immense, less overwhelming, less *constant*. But it was stronger. It was fierce and powerful and desperate and... I wanted it. I wanted the power from that door.

'You feel it just as strongly as the water, Pandora,' Neos said from behind me.

'No,' I said, still staring at the door, letting the heat sear through me. 'No, the water is stronger.' I wanted the words to be true but I didn't know if they were. Water was safer somehow than fire. Fire was... dangerous and passionate, and I was descended from Oceanus. I needed to be one with water. With an effort, I remembered what it had felt like when I became the ocean when I had fought the sea demon. The bliss, the strength, the control. I wrenched my focus from the fire door. I felt cold suddenly, goosebumps raising across my skin.

'Fighting it will not help, little Titan. Very few could be so powerful with opposing elements. You are special, Pandora.' His voice had that seductive quality again, and I found myself stepping towards him, hope filling me. I *needed* to be exceptionally powerful. I needed to be able to get back to my family in the mortal world.

'Can you-' I started to ask him, but broke off the words before I finished them. I couldn't ask a fire demon for help with my powers. Surely that was a bad idea.

He regarded me a long moment, his eyes burning red and a half amused smile on his lips. I kept my mouth clamped shut. I shouldn't be wanting to learn fire magic to make myself more powerful. I should be helping the people whose lives I'd ruined, whose souls I'd caused to be stolen.

'I guess I could let you off your detention today, little Titan. Go and find your ingredients.' I turned and ran towards the library before he could say another word.

'Same time tomorrow, Pandora!' I heard him shout behind me.

9

I jogged straight passed the couches and dove into the shelves of books, moving up and down the bookcases until I spotted Icarus sitting on the floor with a large hardback.

'Hey, you alright?' He jumped to his feet when he saw me, his wings shaking out behind him.

'Yeah,' I panted. 'Neos let me off detention today, to find ingredients.'

Icarus frowned.

'Why would he do that?'

I looked down at my feet, reluctant to answer him.

'I think he knows he scared me a little,' I admitted.

'What? How did he scare you?' Icarus dropped the book as he stepped towards me.

'He didn't do anything bad,' I said quickly. 'It's just... when I'm with him my fire magic is strong. Really strong. The feeling frightened me a bit, that's all.'

'Neos is dangerous,' growled Icarus.

'He's not going to hurt me,' I said, and knew it was true.

'Hmm,' grunted Icarus.

'Did you find anything?' I asked him, changing the subject.

'No,' he shook his head.

I sighed.

'Let's go and get the rust tonight instead,' I said.

'Break into the advanced tower?'

I nodded.

'Yeah. We know it's likely to be in there, and I'm fed up of making no progress at all.'

'OK. Midnight?'

'Midnight,' I agreed.

Icarus was waiting in the shadows as I padded silently to the advanced tower later that night. I had been worried that the teachers would be performing night patrols or being extra vigilant, but the grounds were as empty as they always were at night. I guessed they had faith in the safety potion or were working on their own solution to the demon problem.

There was a padlock on the heavy iron door to the tower and Icarus immediately called a tiny whirlwind of air to his palm. He angled the whirlwind at the lock and closed his eyes as the air entered the lock.

'What are you doing?' I whispered.

'Shhh,' he hissed back. Then there was a click and the padlock fell open. He smiled as he opened his eyes. 'I read about using air to pick locks, if you can solidify it enough,' he grinned.

'Nice trick,' I grinned back.

We pushed open the door with a small creak and slipped inside. I created a little fireball for us to see by, hovering it above our heads. We were in a round entry foyer with the same checkered floor tiles that the front temple had, and a spiral staircase running all the way up and around the stone wall. Doors were set every ten feet or so, spiraling up the tower.

'Wow,' I muttered. 'Which door? There's got to be a hundred in here.'

'They have labels,' said Icarus, squinting at the nearest one. I hurried over, my fireball bringing enough light to read the words above the first door.

'Fangs and Teeth,' read the sign. I ignored my longing to find out what was inside a room named like that, and started up the stairs. Eventually we came to a room labeled 'Wars and the Wounded.'

'This sounds promising,' I said, pausing.

'It sounds morbid,' Icarus muttered back, but carefully pushed open the door. I sent the little fireball in first, slowly, then stepped into the room. A cold uneasiness immediately settled over me, my instincts trying to drag me back out of the room. I ignored them, taking another step inside.

My heart leaped into my throat as I saw movement, but quickly realized that the flickering light was casting eerie shadows over rows and rows of battle armor lining the far wall, making them look as though they were alive. I let out a long breath and tried to steady my nerves.

'Over here,' whispered Icarus. I turned, and saw that he was by a tall cabinet, his own fireball just inches from his face as he peered through the glass. I tip-toed over to him and he pointed to a series of vials containing powders and liquids in a narrow wooden holder. 'It could be one of them?'

'Let's have a look,' I said, and eased the latch on the cabinet door open. I lifted the tiny labels around the neck of each vial and tried to read the swirly handwriting, but the text made no sense to me.

'Can you read that?' I whispered to Icarus. He leaned forward.

'It's in ancient Greek,' he said.

'What does it say?'

'Doxa.'

'What does that mean?'

'Glory.'

'Huh. So this vial gives you glory?' I looked at the dirty looking blue liquid inside. Icarus shrugged.

'Or it came from somebody or something glorious. Either way, it's not what we came here for.'

'These two vials are a reddy-color, they could be rust?' I said, pointing at the two on the right.

'Hang on, I'll look,' he said, and bent over the tiny labels. A slight creaking sound drew my attention back to the door we had come through. We had closed it behind us, and it was still dark and silent and shut. I cast my little fireball over in that direction, adrenaline pumping through me, my eyes roaming the darkness for the source of the creak. The flames flickered off something reflective and I jumped slightly as I saw my own reflection in a suit of armor. It was so highly polished that it looked brand new. I paused my fireball, tilting my head as I watched my reflection. It was *changing*. I was growing taller, and a plumed helmet in rich red was appearing over my head. Leather armor was growing around my body, half covered in an intricate wave pattern, the other half in swirling flames.

'It's this one,' Icarus said behind me, but I barely registered his words.

'Look...' I breathed, my eyes fixed on the warrior version of myself I could see in the breastplate. I stepped towards it.

'Dora, come back,' Icarus hissed, but his words meant nothing to me. The eyes of my reflection were clear now, tiny flames inside my irises, burning fiercely. Power radiated from the figure in the armor, and I gasped as a huge wave roared up behind me in the image. With a tiny smile, reflection me held both palms out. I froze, dimly aware that I hadn't moved my hands, and then the wave rose over the reflections head and burst from the armor.

I gasped as it hit me, cold and hard, then I was tumbling backward, Icarus yelling as I crashed into him and water rushed around us.

'What did you do?'

'I- I just-' I felt him pull me from behind, yanking me to my feet. I turned and grabbed him, then noticed dark green smudges on his arm. 'What's that?'

'I don't know, one of the vials broke when you fell into me.'

'Have you got the rust?' The water was slowing

around us now, but we'd made plenty of noise. We needed to get out of the tower.

'Yes. Can you get rid of the water?'

I concentrated, willing the water away. Slowly it began to dry up. Icarus ran to the door and yanked it open, and we raced down the stairs, the little fireball following behind us. As soon as we were outside we carried on running, towards the pegasus tower, not stopping until we were in the hauler.

'We should go back to our rooms,' panted Icarus. 'They'll know someone was in that tower.'

'They wouldn't look up here,' I gasped. 'And we need to check we got the right thing. How's your arm-' I broke off as I looked down at where the green smudges had been. Icarus's whole forearm was now covered in a patchy dark green substance.

'Dora, why does my arm look like that?' he said slowly, holding his arm out in front of him.

'What did it say on the label on the vial?' I asked.

'I don't know, there were loads of them,' he said, a slight panic in his voice.

'Does it hurt?'

He shook his head.

'It itches a little.'

'OK. We'll wash it off as soon as we can.'

The hauler doors slid open and we stepped out into the corridor.

'Where did all that water come from?' Icarus asked me.

'It was the weirdest thing! There was this armor breastplate and it was really well polished and-'

Icarus crashed to the ground, cutting off my words.

'Icarus!' I yelped, dropping down beside him, barely noticing the impact on my knees. His closed eyes fluttered open and I thought my heart would stop in relief as I saw the shining green color. *It wasn't the soul snatcher.*

'Dora, why are there three of you?' he mumbled. Three of me? I looked at his arm, the green muck snaking its way further up and under his sleeve.

'We need to get that stuff off your arm,' I told him, and tried to pull him to his feet. He was heavy though, and his wings were acting as a dead-weight, dragging him back down every time I tried. 'Who's that?' he said with a half smile, pointing over my shoulder. I whirled, but there was nobody there. 'Hello!' he said cheerfully, and waved.

It was like he was drunk or something. I needed to get the potion off his arm, quickly.

'Wait here,' I told him, and ran down the corridor towards the stables. I leaned over the stable door of the first one to see if the drinking trough had water in it. It did, so I let myself in, talking softly to the dozing pegasus, and picked a bucket up from the corner. The creature flicked its wings a little, then settled back down. I filled the bucket and jogged back to Icarus as carefully as I could, trying not to spill too much.

'Here,' I said, pushing his sleeve up. The green stuff had spread over his shoulder now, and onto his chest and down his back. 'You'll need to take your shirt off.'

'My shirts don't fit anymore,' he told me. 'Since I got proper wings.'

'I know,' I smiled at him, and put my hands hesitantly on the bottom hem of his shirt.

'What are you doing?'

'I need to take off your shirt, Icarus.'

'Oh. They never used to let me wear a shirt.' His eyes darkened as he spoke and he sat up heavily. 'No shirt for the boy with baby wings.'

'Icarus, I'm sorry,' I whispered.

'Not your fault. They used to make me...' He grabbed my arm, his eyes suddenly full of panic.

'Don't let me go back there, Dora, they can't have me! I need to be free!'

My mind flashed on the words of the file I'd seen. *Trapped... Strange experiments...* The fear on his face made my heart ache as he let out a strangled wail.

'It's OK, it's OK, your father's not here now,' I said soothingly, cupping his face with my hands. He stared up at me, wild-eyed. 'Let me wash this stuff off you.' His face went slack suddenly and his arm dropped from mine. I pulled the shirt up over his shoulder, pulling one arm through, and yanked off my own hoodie. I balled it up, dunked it in the bucket and began to slough off the green goo. He said nothing as I worked, but I could hear his heart racing when I leaned close to him. I was careful not to touch his wings, despite wanting to so much. He'd never asked me to, and it somehow didn't feel right to touch them uninvited.

When all the green stuff was off his skin I dropped the hoodie in the bucket and sat down beside him.

'How do you feel?' I asked.

He turned to look at me slowly.

'Better. I could see stuff that I don't think was here and...' He trailed off.

'It must have been a madness potion or something,' I said. He stared at me for a moment.

'How did you know?' he said, quietly.

'Know what?'

'About my father. How did you know about my father?'

My stomach clenched as I looked into his eyes. I couldn't lie to him.

'I saw a file. On Chiron's desk,' I admitted. 'I didn't read all of it but a few sentences caught my eye.'

It was almost as though I could see the walls so painstakingly lifted over the last few weeks slam back down around him. His beautiful eyes hardened and his mouth clenched shut. 'I'm sorry, Icarus, I didn't mean to pry, honestly, it was just right there!'

'What did you read?' His words were barely a whisper.

'That... That your father locked you up and that Hermes rescued you. That's all.'

'That's all?' he repeated, incredulously.

'I didn't mean it like that, oh gods, I'm so sorry!' Tears were filling my eyes and I reached my hand out for him but he pulled his own out of my reach.

'Pandora, I trusted you. Why didn't you tell me you knew something that important about me?'

'I didn't want to force you to talk about it! I wanted you to tell me in your own time. If I could take back what I saw I would, I swear.'

He snorted.

'It's too late for that.' He got to his feet heavily.

'Icarus, please, I'm sorry.'

He stared down at me.

'I need to think,' he said, and stumbled to the hauler.

'I'm sorry,' I repeated, guilt and regret washing over me again and again. He stopped and hope filled me as he turned.

'You'd better take this,' he said, and threw me a small glass vial. I caught it instinctively. It was filled with red powder. The rust. When I looked back up, he was in the hauler. I let the tears spill over my cheeks.

10

The next morning I was awake before Zali for a change. I had barely slept, and my roommate frowned with concern when she saw me.

'Dora, what's wrong? You look...' she trailed off.

'Tired? I'm just tired,' I lied. I had stayed in the pegasus tower late, trying to work out how I could possibly fix what I had done. Icarus needed time, I had accepted, eventually. There was nothing I could do about that. He had spent his life learning not to trust others, being treated badly. And now I had given him a reason not to trust me. I just needed to hope he would understand why I hadn't told him what I knew.

And in the meantime, I couldn't be distracted from the demon, or returning the stolen souls. That *had* to be my priority.

I just didn't know how I was going to do it alone.

· · ·

We were swimming and not flying in first class, so I didn't have to see him. Part of me wanted to, but more of me knew there was nothing I could say and dreaded seeing that cold look he had given me the night before. Being in the water refreshed me, lifting the tired, heavy anxiety from me slightly. The turtles were there, the littlest shooting over to me as soon as Miss Alma gave us permission to go and see them. He headbutted my hand hard when he reached me, his expressive little eyes locking on mine. It was like he knew I'd had a rough night. I smiled at him, and he turned a somersault in the clear blue water. I did the same, our little game cheering me.

Our second lesson was not likely to be so much fun. Agrius stomped onto the training ground, his face serious as ever.

'We're going out,' he barked.

'Out?'

Vronti and Astra stepped up beside him, facing the spear class.

'All first-year students are going on a trip today,' Astra said. Agrius folded his arms sullenly behind her. Excited murmuring rippled through the crowd.

'You'll stay in this group, throughout.' Vronti said. 'And you'll report to Agrius.'

'Where are we going?' Thom asked loudly.

'To the stables on Dionysus's realm, Taurus.'

A thrill shot through me and Tak gave a small exclamation of excitement and grabbed my shoulder.

'Taurean stables! Do you know what kind of animals Dionysus keeps?'

His eyes were alive with excitement and I nodded at him, thinking of my mythology classes.

'Yes! He keeps sphinxes and chimera's and-'

'Calm down, everybody!' Agrius bellowed over the excitement. 'You won't be seeing anything dangerous today, you're first-years. But Hermes has decided it would do you good to go on your first school trip early, so you're going.' He clearly didn't think it was a good idea at all. 'Hermes will be transporting us from the front temple in five minutes, so make your way there now.'

As excited as I was about seeing the creatures in the stables, I was more excited about seeing some of Olympus. Adrenaline skittered through me as I followed the crowd through the main temple, half-listening to Tak listing the animals he hoped we would see. Would we see Dionysus? Taurus was the tree-house realm. Much as I loved the underwater academy, the thought of being in a forest, of seeing a *tree* for the first time in months, was filling me with joy.

And boy was I right to be excited.

When we reached the front temple, Hermes clicked his fingers and suddenly we were surrounded by trees. And the trees on Taurus were not just any trees. They were *massive*. I gaped as I craned my neck, trying to take everything in. Dark brown trunks rose from the earthy forest floor we were standing on, and wooden huts rested in the long, sturdy branches. The huts were painted with bright swirling patterns, some even carved into the trunks of the trees, and tiny dancing fairy lights illuminated the areas shaded by enormous green leaves. I breathed in deeply, inhaling the smell of earth, and listened to the rustling sound of leaves and cracking of twigs. The heat from the rays of light filtering down through the forest canopy warmed my face and felt amazing.

'Welcome to Taurus,' a female voice said, and we all looked to our left. A slight lady, probably in her twenties and barely five feet tall, was smiling at us. She wore a beautiful flowing white gown and a silver circlet entwined with delicate green leaves topped her warm brown hair. 'I am Princess Morea, of House Augeas.' I let out a breath and glanced at Tak. He grinned back at me. A real-life princess?

'The princess will show us to the royal stables,' grunted Agrius. 'Stay in groups, don't wander off, and do what you're told.'

The princess smiled at him and gestured towards a tree trunk as wide as my house.

'Make your way over here, please.' We all moved, eagerly, towards the tree.

'Is this the palace?' somebody near Princess Morea asked.

'No. These huts are part of the Kingdom of Augeas. The palace is much higher up in the trees,' she answered softly.

'Can we see it?'

She gave a tinkling laugh and Agrius snorted.

'Do you know how hard it is to get an invite into a Taurean palace?' he said, rolling his eyes. 'Good luck with that.'

The princess raised an eyebrow at him and turned back to the student.

'Invitations are exclusive, that is true. But you must always have hope. One never knows.' Her eyes shone. She turned to the tree trunk and said something in a language I didn't understand and then an oblong shape began to glow in the wood, forming a door.

'We have many creatures here, and they are all unpredictable so please follow the rules. Do not enter the pens. Do not tap or shout or otherwise disturb the animals. And do not use magic around them.'

Everybody nodded.

'Everyone back here in one hour,' called Agrius, and we followed Princess Morea into the tree.

'The animal's pens line the outside of the tree trunk in a ring,' the princess explained as we walked through the dimly lit woody corridor. 'We view them from the middle of the tree so that we are safely inside and they are out there.' That made sense, I thought. 'The most dangerous creatures are kept elsewhere, these are just the ones my father, the king, wishes to display today.' I thought about zoos back at home, and hoped the animals didn't mind being kept here, on display. As if hearing my thought the princess continued. 'They are given free run of the forest floor at night, and return of their own volition during the day, for feeding. They are well cared for.' She slowed and spoke another word in the strange language. The bark making up the wall around us began to lift and I gasped as glass was revealed behind it. We were standing next to a huge pen, which looked a lot like a lion enclosure. Everyone, including myself, began scanning the pen for an animal.

'It is important to remember that many of the creatures we keep here have evolved forms now, that live a sentient life among the citizens of Olympus. We only keep wild, un-evolved creatures here. So whilst there are many harpies, or griffins or telkhines that live in Olympus as our equals, there are just as many who live in the wild, unaware of their evolved counterparts.'

There was a thud and my attention was pulled from the princess and back on the pen. A huge animal was jumping down from where it had been concealed in a winding leafy tree. Though it had the body and limbs of a lion, it had the head of a mean looking eagle. A hooked yellowing beak jutted out under hard black eyes and shining tan wings beat out from it's back.

'This is a griffon,' Princess Morea said. I watched it, transfixed as it stalked up to the glass, cocking its head. 'Feel free to walk around, and look at the others. I'll be here if you have any questions.'

'Come on!' said Tak, pulling my arm as students hurried off in either direction, keeping a healthy few feet from the glass.

I let him pull me along to the next pen, then slowed to see what was inside. It was filled with sand and looked empty except for a dusty stone structure at the back. We watched the dark doorway in the stone hut but nothing happened.

'I can't believe we're here, on Taurus,' I said as we watched.

'I can't believe we might see a sphinx!' Tak replied. Eventually the two students still watching and waiting with us sighed loudly and moved on. S'pose we should give up on this one,' Tak said.

'I guess so.'

We walked quickly onto the next pen and I let out a little gasp involuntarily. It was filled with water halfway up the glass, and steam was blowing gently off the surface. Stretched out on the dry and dark rocky bank of the pool was the ugliest thing I'd ever seen. It looked sort of like a dog, except that it had flippers ending in weird webbed hands, and a tail like a seal. It was dozing, matted fur running down its bony back.

'What is that?' I breathed.

'Telkhine!' Tak said excitedly. 'The evolved ones work in Hephaestus's forges and make really cool stuff for the gods, like Hades' invisibility helmet.'

'Hades has an invisibility helmet?'

'Yeah. How do you not know that?' Tak shook his head at me in disbelief. 'Anyway, they're really amazing metal-workers.'

I squinted at the thing's webbed fingers.

'How?'

Tak shrugged.

'I dunno,' he said. 'They just are.'

.   .   .

We carried on around the trunk of the tree, seeing creatures in about half of the pens, most of them sleeping. There was a pegasus three times the size of Peto, it's enormous white wings filling the pen as it lay sleeping in the middle of the stall, and I couldn't help wondering how happy it was in such a small space. Eventually we came back to the griffin, pacing up and down along the glass.

'What do you think of the stables?' the princess asked us.

'They're great!' Tak beamed. She smiled at him and looked at me.

'I... Um....' I wasn't sure what to say. They were incredible, sure, but the pens just seemed so *small*. 'Do they have enough space?' I blurted out. Tak froze beside me and Princess Morea raised her eyebrows.

'Yes, of course they do. I'll show you,' she said, and beckoned us to follow her. Tak elbowed me as we set off, glaring at me. I guess you weren't supposed to challenge a member of the royal family. 'Here,' she said, stopping before the empty sand-filled pen with the stone structure at the back. She put her hand against the glass and whispered inaudibly. Something moved inside the stone den. 'This is Sting. He's Dionysus's pet manticore.' My heart began to hammer in my chest as a sleek maneless lion slunk out of the den. Would this be my chance to get a manticore feather? Huge black claws ringed the front of its paws and behind it rose a scale-plated tail ending in a glowing red stinger, like a scorpion's. 'He's rare as manticores usually have wings.'

No wings. My excitement died instantly.

'So no feathers then,' I said quietly. The princess turned to me with a small frown.

'No. But he can leave whenever he wants. Through the back of that stone den. But he chooses not to. The creatures are not unhappy here.'

The manticore's eyes met mine through the glass and he flicked his tongue lazily out of his mouth, showing me his razor sharp teeth as he prowled closer. The red stinger pulsed with a glowing light.

'He's beautiful,' I said.

'He is, isn't he?' the princess sighed, turning away from me and looking fondly towards Sting. 'And clever, for a wild beast.'

'What does he eat?' asked Tak, enthusiastically.

'Meat,' she answered simply, giving him a sideways look.

'Oh,' he replied, clearly hoping for a more gory answer. A thought occurred to me.

'Are there other manticores here?' I asked.

'Yes. Two, actually. They sleep during the day, so I'm not surprised you didn't see them.'

'Do *they* have wings?' I asked hopefully.

'Yes...' she answered, brown eyes crinkling as she peered at me. 'Why?'

'I need a manticore feather,' I said quickly.

'You need what?' repeated Tak, screwing his face up.

'For Advanced Magical Objects,' I lied fast. None of my friends were in that class with me so it was an easy lie to tell.

Princess Morea cocked her head, regarding me.

'A manticore feather can be used for many things, I

believe,' she said. 'I attended the academy too, you know,' she added with a small smile.

'Really?' Tak stared at her.

'Of course. Not the one you're at, royals and nobles are sent somewhere more...' she paused. 'Comfortable,' she finished. 'But I remember Potions and Magical Objects classes. What do you want with a manticore feather?'

I swallowed as Tak turned to me too.

'Nothing, in particular. I just read they could be useful,' I said, as casually as I could.

'Hmmmm,' she said. 'Well, it just so happens that one of the manticore stalls will be empty and open for cleaning in a few minutes. Your class is due to leave at the same time though. But... if a student were quick enough and they knew that it was exactly five stalls on the right from here, they might be able to sneak in and grab a fallen feather...' She gave me a quick wink, and strode off before I could thank her.

I turned right, in the direction she had said the pen was.

'What's going on?' Tak said, coming after me as I began jogging down the corridor.

'Nothing, I just really want a feather.'

'Well, I guess they're pretty cool, but worth being late and getting in trouble with Agrius for?'

Getting my hands on another one of the ingredients for the potion was *so* worth getting in trouble with Agrius for, but I couldn't tell Tak that. I shrugged instead.

'Why not? He already hates me.'

'That's true.'

11

We slowed when we reached the pen five doors down. There were no other students around now, as they were all heading back to the meeting point outside the tree. As I watched, the glass in front of the stall lifted, slowly.

'Are you sure about this? What if the manticore is still in there?' Tak said apprehensively.

'Then they wouldn't open it, with students still here,' I said and took a few steps closer. 'Stay here and watch out for whoever is coming to clean it.'

'OK,' he answered, looking up and down the corridor.

My nose scrunched up as I got close, the smell of animal much more potent than the pegasus stables I had gotten used to. The stall had a sprawling tree up one wall, the same as the griffon enclosure, and a series of large, sandy rocks on the other side. There was a rocky cave at the back, the mouth dark and still. When I was sure I couldn't see any movement I stepped through from the corridor, onto the sand. I began to scan the floor, looking for feathers. There were small rocks, and things that looked suspiciously like bones, and a few leaves and lumps of mud and dirt, but I couldn't see any feathers. I moved over to the base of the tree, looking up at the branches, hopeful that a feather may have become caught when the creature was climbing. To my disappointment though, I could only see green leaves. Then, suddenly, there was a loud clicking sound and I jerked my head around in time to see the glass front of the pen slamming back down to the floor. I froze, unsure what was happening. Why had the pen door shut? And where was Tak?

I waited a few seconds, looking for Tak in the corridor beyond the glass, but he had gone. All I saw was a flash of silver disappearing around the bend. Astra or Vronti, the silver-haired twins? A rustle from behind me made me whirl again and then my blood turned to ice in my veins. Red eyes were glowing from inside the cave.

Fear washed through me as one giant paw emerged, and my eyes glued to the lethally sharp black claws. How was the manticore still in here? The pen had been open! I took a shaky step backward. I needed to get out. I needed help. I took another step, quicker, as a horned lion head followed the paw out of the cave. I gave a small, involuntary cry as my back bumped against the glass and the creature froze, its eyes locked on mine. Too frightened to take my eyes off the manticore, I knocked my fist on the glass behind me, lightly at first, then harder as the beast resumed its slow prowl towards me. When it emerged from the cave fully my breath caught in realization. It didn't have wings.

'Sting?' I whispered. It paused again, cocking its head slightly. 'How did you get in here?' I murmured, trying to keep my voice from shaking, still knocking on the glass. I had no idea if anybody was on the other side of it. Surely Tak had gone for help?

The manticore's eyes flicked to my hands and the flashing scorpion stinger rose high above his back as he bared his teeth. I froze, stopping the knocking. The stinger lowered, and the snarling lessened.

'OK. I won't do that then,' I breathed. 'Why aren't you outside, in the forest?' I said, trying to use the same soothing voice I used when I was talking to Peto. The beast took a slow step closer to me, unblinking. I darted a glance up at the tree. Could I get up there before him? Doubtful, I thought. He would be much quicker at climbing than me. Sting took another step, now less than ten feet from me. 'You don't want to eat me,' I said, giving him a weak smile. 'Surely you've already been fed today?' Please, please gods, let him have been fed today, I prayed. Maybe I could get around him, to the cave and out that way? He took another step.

Adrenaline was coursing through me now, but the room was dry and my power wasn't surging around inside me like it did in the underwater academy. I was aware of the water in the telkhine pen a few stalls over, but I couldn't get it out of that pen and use it. Could I conjure enough up from nothing to be useful? Heat tingled across my skin as Sting took another long stride. He was five feet away now, his massive head and flashing red eyes fixed on me. I held up a shaking hand, calling up a fireball. It burst to life above me and Sting stopped, his cat eyes moving to crackling ball.

The princess's words rang in my mind. *Do not use magic around the creatures.* Had I broken royal rules? What would happen to me if I wasn't eaten by Sting? Surely these were exceptional circumstances, I thought desperately, as the manticore dropped his gaze from the fireball and settled back on me. He lifted a paw from the ground, closing the gap between us even further. I was sweating now, both from fear and the building heat starting to engulf me. I willed the fireball above me bigger, but Sting didn't look at it. I didn't want to hurt him, I really didn't. But...

'Woah! Woah, you don't want to do that!' A well-spoken male voice rang across the room and Sting flicked his head around to the cave. An older boy, with soft brown hair and warm brown eyes crawled out of it, a large sack hanging from his left hand. 'If he wanted to, that stinger would have killed you from back here. If you throw a fireball at him, he'll *definitely* kill you.'

'I'm pretty sure he's going to eat me anyway,' I whispered.

'Nah, he doesn't eat humans when he can have what I've got here,' he grinned, waving the sack at the manticore. Sting looked between me and the sack, then turned towards the boy. He pulled a huge lump of raw flesh from the bag and launched it up onto the highest of the big sandy rocks. I held my breath as the stinger swung in front of me as the manticore bounded after the meat, leaping the distance easily. The fireball fizzled out as I sagged in relief.

'See?' grinned the boy, as Sting dropped down flat to the rocks, his huge teeth sinking into the meat. 'Good job I'm on cleaning duty today though, anybody else might have let him play with you. What are you doing in here?'

'I... I got trapped in here. The glass was open,' I stammered, pressing my sweaty palms flat against the glass behind me. That had been way, *way* too close.

'Huh. Sting is supposed to be locked in his stall when students are here,' he frowned. 'Oh well, no harm done. Come on. If you're with the last class, they were supposed to leave already.' He held his hand out to me and I pushed myself nervously off the glass, looking at Sting. 'Don't worry, he'll ignore you,' the boy said. And he did, completely, as I crept across the room and gripped the boy's hand with relief.

'Who are you?' I asked as he pulled me into the dark cave.

'Prince Phyleus,' his voice came back as we crawled through the dark. 'You probably met my sister earlier.'

'Prince?' I half yelped, my voice echoing off the rock.

He laughed.

'Yeah. Don't worry, I won't tell anybody what happened. I'm always in trouble too,' he said as light began to filter around us and I saw the cave exit.

We emerged onto the dirty forest floor and stood up quickly. I pulled my hand back awkwardly and brushed at my bare knees, scuffed and scraped from the stone of the cave.

'Well, thank you, very much, for saving me,' I said in my most formal voice, unable to meet his eyes.

'No worries. Maybe be more careful around lethal wild animals in future,' he said cheerfully. I raised my gaze to his. He was grinning. 'Your class is supposed to meet round the other side of the tree. You'd better hurry.'

I nodded.

'Thank you,' I said again, and ran towards where he was pointing.

I met Tak's relieved expression when I rounded the giant tree trunk with a glare. Guilt washed over his face and he opened his mouth as I slowed to a stop beside him, the rest of the class hovering in a group, looking over at me and muttering.

'Pandora?' roared Agrius, before Tak could speak. I winced. 'Where have you been? I told everyone to meet here ten minutes ago! That included you!'

I turned as the angry man stomped towards me, the other students scattering. Astra and Vronti were both staring at me, cold and expressionless.

'I... Um... I got lost,' I said, lamely.

Agrius glared down at me.

'Detention. Laps of the training ground after your last class.'

I cut off my groan before it fully escaped, the teacher's eyes flashing with anger.

'Yes, professor,' I said instead, glaring back.

. . .

'Where in Zeus's name were you?' I hissed at Tak as soon as Agrius had stamped off.

'I don't know what happened! I was keeping lookout, like you said, then I heard your voice, calling me from down the corridor. When I looked back in the pen I couldn't see you, so I followed the voice and then I was being gathered up with the other students by Agrius and the princess. Honestly, Dora, I'm so sorry.' His beseeching eyes told me he wasn't lying and I relaxed my glare.

'Somebody tricked you,' I snarled. 'And I think it was one of them.' I nodded towards the Zeus twins.

'Astra and Vronti? Nah, they're too well-behaved. What happened anyway? Did you get the feather?'

'No,' I sighed, looking at him. 'I'll tell you what happened at dinner, when Zali and-' I hesitated, thinking about Icarus. Would he sit with us at dinner? I doubted it. 'When Zali and the others are there,' I finished. 'Although I'm not sure you'll believe me.'

12

Once Hermes had flashed us back to the academy, we were told it was too late for lunch in the main temple and given sandwiches to take to our next class. I got a few angry glares from the others for costing them their lunch break, and I kept my head down apologetically.

In Advanced Magical Objects we went through methods of spotting cursed objects, and though I would normally be interested, I couldn't focus on what Professor Fantasma was saying. Who had trapped me in that pen? And had they known Sting was loose or was that a coincidence? It couldn't have been an accident, I reasoned. Somebody had lured Tak away. And how had he not seen me or the glass front close? It would take strong telepathy powers to do that. My eyes fell on Astra, who was paying close attention to the teacher. I was *sure* I'd seen silver. And the twins were excellent at telepathy, and every other class for that matter. But they had no reason to try to hurt me. If anybody wanted to trap me in a pen with a manticore it would be Arketa.

My last class was Water and I concentrated on staying out of everyone's way and not drenching anybody. Adrenaline still hummed through me and I didn't trust myself to open up to the water surrounding us. Dasko frowned a little at my tiny whirlpools when he came to see how I was doing, but thankfully he didn't push me.

'Attention, please,' he called, near the end of the lesson. 'Your second semester exams are going to be overseen by Hermes in two months.'

Well, at least Zeus wasn't coming this time.

'I know we've had a bit of a shock start to this semester but the Gods are keen to continue the high level of expectation at the academy. Anybody who fails too many exams will be asked to leave.'

My skin seemed to tighten across my body as anxiety rippled through me. *Leave and go and wander the mortal world alone forever.* I couldn't fail.

'If you need any extra help, please do ask your teachers. It's what we're here for,' he finished. His eyes settled on mine. His meaning was clear. I needed more help. The gong sounded and I blew out a sigh as the other students grabbed their bags and began filing out of the room. I trudged over to Dasko.

'I guess I need more extra classes,' I mumbled.

'I'm free again this Sunday if you are,' he smiled at me.

'Yeah. Sure,' I sighed. Dasko looked over at the last student leaving the water room.

'Don't be so down about it Pandora, you only need the extra classes because you have the potential to be so powerful. It's a good thing.'

'It doesn't feel like it,' I grumbled. 'And all the other students still hate me.' I thought about telling him that I thought one of them tried to kill me earlier, but decided it sounded too dramatic. I didn't actually know it wasn't an accident.

'Just work hard, and it'll pay off,' he said. His eyes were soft and reassuring.

'I will,' I said. 'And thank you. For giving up your time for me.'

'You're welcome.'

When I got to the training ground for my detention with Agrius he was already there, launching spears at a massive practice target.

'You're late again, Pandora,' he spat.

'I was talking with Professor Dasko,' I answered.

'Get changed and give me twenty laps,' he grunted. I glared at his huge back as he turned back to the target, then trudged off to the changing rooms.

I was starving by the time I'd finished running in circles around the training ground. I didn't even change out of my running clothes, just headed straight into the main temple, praying for hot dogs. I faltered slightly as I reached our usual place at the dining table, Icarus's absence was like a punch to the gut. Maybe he was just late, like me, I thought, but I knew deep down that he wasn't coming.

'Dora! Tak was telling us about what happened earlier, we're desperate to hear the rest!' Zali exclaimed when she saw me. I sat down beside her and she frowned. 'Why haven't you changed?'

'Too hungry,' I said, and leaned over, piling bread buns and sausages onto my plate.

'Where's Icarus?' asked Tak, looking about.

'We, um, had a fight,' I mumbled, not looking at him.

'Really? About what?'

'It doesn't matter. He's just taking a bit of time. To think.' My voice choked a little and I picked up a hot dog and shoved it in my mouth, before I or anyone else could say any more.

Tak opened his mouth to speak but Zali cut him off quickly.

'So, the manticore pen, what happened? And why do you want a feather?'

Between mouthfuls I told them about Sting and my close call.

'A prince? You met an actual prince? Gods, Dora, you're so lucky!' squealed Zali when I'd finished.

'Lucky?' I gaped at her. 'Did you hear the bit where I thought I was going to be eaten alive?'

'But a prince rescued you! It's just so perfect!'

'Zali, there is nothing perfect about my life right now,' I grumbled.

'Yeah, what's so good about princes?' scowled Tak. 'And who tricked me and closed the glass?'

I shrugged.

'I don't know. The only person here who hates me enough to do that is Arketa.'

'Could it have been her?'

'I didn't see her. And I don't think her telepathy is good enough to hide me from Tak.'

We all fell quiet as Professor Neos strode over to our table. Students fell silent around us as he smiled around at them.

'Pandora,' he said, stopping opposite me.

Oh gods. I'd missed my detention with him, I realized, my stomach lurching.

'I was in detention with Agrius,' I spluttered.

He quirked an eyebrow.

'That's a lot of detentions, young lady.'

'I know,' I ground out.

'One more weeks worth should make up for not showing up.'

I gaped at him.

'But-' I started, but he smiled at me and strolled off, towards the teachers' table on the dais.

I groaned, closing my eyes.

'How am I going to do anything between detention every night for two weeks and Dasko's extra class on Sunday?'

'Well, there's not much else to do now but study,' said Zali sympathetically. 'Only two months until next exams.'

'Yeah, I'm getting some extra classes in with Fantasma,' Tak said. We talked a while about the exams, and I felt a bit better that I wasn't the only one having to put in extra time. After dinner I excused myself and went straight into the bookshelves, to the section on Scorpio. I still hadn't found any information on fire rafes. I was hoping Icarus might be there too, but there was no sign of him. I hadn't seen his big black wings anywhere in the temple at dinner and I couldn't help feeling worried about him. If he said he needed time, then that's what I would give him, I told myself. Trouble was, patience was definitely *not* one of my virtues.

13

I struck lucky on the third book about Scorpio I opened.

Fire rafes grow in warm water and are very beautiful, very dangerous plants.

I read on, my tired eyes suddenly perking up as they took in the picture of a plant covered in stunning orange and red flowers, shaded like fierce flames.

They are rare due to the short amount of time they bloom for. Once planted, they need four weeks to grow and will then only bloom for exactly twelve hours, before bursting into underwater flames and ceasing to exist.

. . .

My hopes sank to the pit of my stomach like a stone. Twelve hours? I had to get underneath the school and look for a rare plant that only existed for twelve hours? I let out a long, unhappy sigh. This was not going to be easy.

'Are you OK, Dora?' Zali asked me when I trudged into our dorm room.

'Yeah. Tired from all the excitement on Taurus,' I said.

'And... Icarus?' she prompted, coming to sit beside me on my bed. I saw the concern on her face and tears pricked at my eyes.

'I let him down,' I whispered, trying to hold them back.

'Oh Dora, I'm sure you didn't,' my friend said, throwing her arms around me.

'I did, Zali. I lied to him.'

'About what?'

'Stuff I should have been honest about,' I mumbled into her curly hair.

She pulled away and looked at me for a moment.

'I'm sure you had a good reason,' she said eventually, with a small nod.

'You have too much faith in me,' I told her, a tear escaping.

'Don't be silly. I know you're a good person. So if you lied, it was for a reason. He'll realize that, I'm sure.'

'Oh, I hope so,' I told her, praying the words were true.

'He will. You wait, he'll be back sitting with us for dinner by tomorrow.'

But he wasn't. And he wasn't there for lunch the day after that either. Gida joined us though, and he was chatting about a plan he and some older students were devising to bait the Keres demon by not drinking the safety potion. I had only been half listening, scanning the temple for Icarus's wings, but when I realized what he was saying, I gave him my full attention.

'Isn't that really dangerous?' I said.

'Well, yeah, course it is,' the satyr said, puffing his chest out. 'But we're the most advanced students here. Most only spend two years at the academy. We've been here nearly four.'

'How are you going to stop it when it comes though?' asked Zali, her face a mask of worry.

'We're making a potion that means we'll be able to see it, so we can stop it before it gets to us,' he said.

I frowned, wondering if it was anything like the potion we were trying to make. Would they really be brave enough to not drink their safety potions? What if more people were hurt, or lost their souls?

'I think it sounds too risky. There must be a better way to bait it than not drinking the safety potion,' I said.

The satyr shrugged.

'Yeah, loads, but this is the easiest and most likely to work.'

I thought about the note from Neos with the list of ingredients for the baiting potion. Should I share it with the others? If they were going to try to catch the demon, shouldn't they have this information too? I would ask Neos, I decided.

'How are you going to kill it? Will that bring the souls back?' Tak asked.

'That's the bit we haven't worked out yet,' Gida answered. 'Bit more research to do.'

Neos had said that a powerful god could convince Hades to return the souls if they had the demon. Was there any other way to kill it and return the souls? I found myself hoping against hope that Gida and the older students would find something out in their research, that there was an easier, safer way.

'Keep us updated,' I said.

The gong rang for the next lesson and Tak, Zali and I all got up together to go to History of Mythology. My stomach fluttered nervously. I would see Icarus now, for sure. We made our way to the blue curtained door, and when I entered the classroom I saw his black wings immediately. He was sitting on the far side of the room, not looking at anybody who came in. Nobody was sat next to him. Emotion skittered through me and I crushed the urge to go over to him. *He'd asked for time.* Tak glanced at me, paused, then went towards Icarus. I watched as Tak clapped him on the back and sat down beside him, and Icarus gave him a sideways look and a grunt.

'They can have some boy-time,' said Zali, and gently tugged me towards the back of the classroom. I tried not to be hurt that Icarus wouldn't even look at me. I tried not to care that he found it so easy to not even glance towards me. But I couldn't stop the sadness that settled over me.

'Hello, class. We're going to talk about punishments of the gods today,' said Dasko, strolling through the curtain and to the front of the room. 'It is important that we all understand that whether it is right or wrong, the gods are able to mete out any punishment they like, even if the crime doesn't appear to deserve it.'

I pulled out my notepad.

'Now, Zeus is Lord of the Olympians, as you know. And he... well he doesn't always behave as his wife, Hera, wishes he would. He has been known to draw attention to himself by spending too much time with women who are *not* his wife. And Hera has come up with some interesting ways to punish those women over the years. In an attempt to hide one woman, named Io, from Hera, Zeus turned her into a cow. But Hera knew what he was up to and sent a gadfly to bite the cow all day, every day, until Io was so sleep deprived and uncomfortable she nearly went mad.'

I scratched at an imaginary itch on my shoulder, scrunching up my nose.

'And many mortals have regretted suggesting they were better at something than the gods were. Actaeon believed he was a better hunter than Artemis. She made his own hunting dogs eat him. Arachne believed she was a better weaver than Athena. After winning a competition set by the muses, Athena turned her into a spider.

Marsyas challenged Apollo to a lute playing competition, and upon losing was flayed alive.'

I squirmed uncomfortably in my seat and wrote 'Gods are better at everything' on the notepad page.

'But I think the most deserved of all the famous punishments was Tantalus.'

The fire dish in the center of the room burst to life, showing a well-dressed man in a toga, beaming.

'Tantalus was a demigod, a son of Zeus in fact, and he was fortunate enough to get himself an invite to dine with the Olympians. But Tantalus was not a nice man. He wanted to test the gods because he didn't believe that they knew everything. So he killed his own son, and made a stew with his body.'

I wasn't the only person in the classroom to gasp at Dasko's words. Zali looked at me, horror on her pretty face.

'He served the stew to the gods but, of course, they knew what he had done. Zeus condemned Tantalus's kingdom, then forced him to stand in a pool of water in the underworld for eternity. Every time he tries to drink from the pool, the water recedes to nothing. He is standing under a tree, ripe with fresh fruit, and every time he tries to pick the fruit it leaps from his reach. He will be hungry and thirsty forever, never quite able to reach the things that would quench his needs.'

My eyes were fixed on the flame dish, showing an old, stooped man, trying desperately to catch water in his hands from a pool around him, but the water drained to nothing each time he tried.

'How awful,' Zali whispered.

'He did kinda deserve it though,' I whispered back.

'Sisyphus and Ixion also serve endless torture in Hades' realm. I want you to get into pairs and look through your books about Virgo and find out what each of them did to upset Zeus.'

'Did the gods eat the stew?' a boy in the first row asked loudly.

'No, of course not,' Dasko said, shaking his head. 'Well, Demeter accidentally ate a little bit, as she was distracted. But Zeus brought the boy back to life, and apart from a small part of his elbow, he was fine.'

'Well, that's good,' whispered Zali, her face still slightly pale.

Icarus didn't sit with us for the rest of the week. My heart ached whenever I spotted him sitting alone at another table, his big wings wrapped around him like a shield. I wanted so badly to go and talk to him, but I needed to prove to him that I could respect his request. Plus, I didn't want to force a confrontation that would end in him never forgiving me. So instead, I tried to concentrate on getting the potion ingredients and controlling my elemental powers. My detentions with Neos were turning out to be more useful than scary when it came to my fire magic.

If I could ignore the fact that he was a demon, he was actually a really good teacher. He'd not tried to scare me again, instead starting each detention with a tiny flame in the dish in the middle of the fire classroom. He explained how fire didn't work like water, running in continuous and solid patterns, but that it was erratic and unpredictable. Water existed in designated quantities, whereas fire could grow and shrink. Water had to be summoned from somewhere, which was hard unless you had a lot of power, but fire could be snapped into existence from anywhere, just by drawing on the air always present around us.

The more he explained the differences between the two, the more the fire magic made sense. Where water's disadvantages lay, fire's advantages stood out. We practiced making fireballs no larger than the size of soccer balls, guiding them around the room and shrinking them as they flew about, and my underlying fear of the flames lessened.

'Now that the other students know about the death demon, can we tell them about the bait potion?' I asked Neos at the end of our detention on Friday.

'No, I don't think that's a good idea,' he answered quickly.

'Why not?'

'Because you would have students all over the school baiting the demon and risking their souls. You wouldn't want that, would you?'

'If they've drunk the safety potion it wouldn't be a problem would it?'

'The safety potion only protects their souls. Death demons have other ways of doing damage, Pandora,' he said seriously.

'Like how?' I asked, alarmed.

'They can attack your mind, or immobilize your body, or sometimes even possess others.'

'What?' Fear thrummed through me at his words. 'So we're not safe at all?'

'The Keres is after souls. She wouldn't do any of those things if there wasn't a chance of getting one, unless she had a good reason - like being attacked.'

'How are *we* going to catch her then?' I asked. 'It sounds impossible!'

'Not if you have another demon on your side,' he answered with a grin, his red eyes flashing.

14

'There we go,' said Zali, pinning a tiny braid of my hair to the twist of others she'd done.

'It looks amazing, thank you,' I told her.

'You're welcome. Icarus will *have* to talk to you looking like that,' she beamed. My stomach flipped. I had been dreading the school dance all day. The last few had been so much fun, dancing with Icarus, his wings curling around us. Now I didn't know if he would even look at me. I didn't want to go at all but Zali was insisting.

'I don't think he'll care much what I look like,' I said.

'Try talking to him then,' she said softly.

'I can't. He said he needed time to think.'

'Hmmm. Boys shouldn't be left to think too long. They'll come to all sorts of silly conclusions without some female input,' she said.

When we entered the main temple there was a lively tune playing, a loud drum beat resounding off the marble columns, but not many people were dancing. I saw Arketa and Filis standing together, barely speaking. Their normal aura of beauty and poise was somehow missing and they didn't look right without Kiko, I thought. She may have been just as nasty as they were, but she hadn't deserved what had happened to her. And her friends clearly missed her.

'There's Tak,' said Zali, and we headed over to where he was chatting to Thom.

'I heard you got into trouble on Taurus,' he said to me as we reached them.

'Oh, I, um,' I stammered. Nobody *ever* spoke to me or Icarus, apart from Zali, Tak and Gida.

'Good job you got out safely, I've heard manticores can be pretty dangerous,' he said playfully. He *was* a manticore shifter.

'Yeah, he was pretty scary,' I said carefully.

'I know, I saw him when we visited. He's called Sting, right?'

I nodded.

'Well, I don't think there are many evolved manticores in Olympus. He's about as trained as they come. Tak said you were really interested in manticores?'

'I am, yeah,' I said, throwing Tak a look. He shrugged, eyes sparkling.

'Well, I'd be happy to talk to you about them. I've had to do loads of research, obviously.'

'Really?' I looked at him in surprise and he smiled.

'Sure,' he said, pushing his brown hair back from his face. I scanned it, looking for signs he was teasing me or about to follow up with a nasty joke or trick. He'd never been nasty to me before though. 'Not many people are into manticores,' he said eventually, with a shrug. 'Nice to find someone that is.'

He really *did* want to talk to me, I realized. I felt a flash of guilt that I wasn't actually that interested in the creatures, that I just needed a feather, but I smiled back at him. It wasn't like it was a boring subject to talk about.

'That would be great,' I said. 'Thanks.'

'Sure. You got a drink yet?'

I shook my head, my heart skipping a little. I hadn't expected to be making new friends tonight.

'I'll go grab us some.' He turned, heading off towards the punch fountain.

'Tak!' I hissed, turning towards him. 'Why did you tell him I was into manticores?'

'Well you were determined to go in that pen and get a feather,' he protested, holding both his hands up. 'I assumed you were!'

I rolled my eyes.

'He's nice,' said Zali. 'Talking to him can't hurt.'

She was right. Why was I so nervous?

'Pandora?' I whirled, coming face to face with Icarus.

'Icarus,' I breathed, stepping towards him. He held a drink out to me awkwardly.

'Oh, thank you,' I said, taking it. 'How are you?' I asked, fixing my gaze on those intense emerald green eyes, my tummy turning somersaults.

'Alright,' he shrugged, his dark hair flopping forward. 'How are you?'

I shrugged too.

'OK,' I said.

'Any luck with the potion?' he asked, looking around hesitantly.

I shook my head.

'No. But I did find out some stuff about fire rafes,' I said. My heart was hammering against my chest now. I didn't want to talk about the potion. I wanted to ask him if he had forgiven me.

'Oh. That's good,' he said.

'Yeah.'

'I heard you had some trouble on Taurus?'

'Oh, yeah, I was trying to get a manticore feather,' I said.

'Did you get it?'

'No.'

We lapsed into awkward silence.

'Pandora,' Thom's voice came from behind me and he held out a glass of punch as I turned to him. 'Oh, hi,' he said to Icarus.

Icarus's green eyes darted between me and Thom as I took the second drink.

'Thom's talking to me about manticores,' I said quickly.

'Right. Well, see you later,' he said and turned from me before I could open my mouth.

'Wait!' I said, taking a step after him, but his wings disappeared into the crowd as he moved quickly away. I clenched my teeth as I gripped both glasses, frustration welling in me.

'Did I interrupt something?' asked Thom.

I closed my eyes, took a long breath, then turned back to him with a smile.

'No, it's fine,' I said. 'So, are manticore wings always the same color?' I asked him.

'No, not at all,' he said excitedly, and started to tell me all about the various colors the feathers could be. I would build up to asking him where I might find a feather, I thought. If tonight was a total bust with Icarus, then I had to at least make some progress with the potion.

Listening to Thom talk animatedly about the creatures was actually a lot more fun than I thought it would be. His passion for the subject was infectious, and he knew so much interesting stuff. Before I knew it, I'd drained both glasses and had a burning desire to study manticores myself.

'Course, if you stay here three years you can specialize in mythical beasts. Then you get to work with some really cool stuff, like dragons and chimeras.'

'Dragons?'

'Yeah, snakey lizardy things with big wings.'

I laughed.

'I know what a dragon is! I just didn't know you had them in Olympus.'

'Oh yeah, I forget you're from the mortal world.'

'Where are you from?'

'Cancer.'

'That's Hera's realm?' I asked.

'Yup. It's real nice. All forest and lakes and big white stone houses.'

'How did your parents react when you found out what your power was?' I asked tentatively.

'My older brother was a manticore shifter too, so not that surprised,' he grinned. 'Off to the academy I went.'

'Oh, cool,' I answered, trying to imagine how different his childhood would have been from mine.

'So, what do you want to do with your powers? Do you want to stay at the academy and specialize in something?'

'Um...' I said. What I really wanted to do was become powerful enough to get back home to my dad and Mandy. But beyond that... I really wasn't sure anymore. 'I want to see Olympus,' I answered eventually. 'It sounds incredible.'

'It is, but it's only safe to see about half of it. I'd love to see one of the forbidden realms.'

'Me too,' I said.

His eyes shone as he looked at me and I couldn't help smiling. His enthusiasm was nice.

'Do you, um, want to dance?' he said, eyes darting from mine to the dance floor.

'Oh, I, um, well, um...' I spluttered, genuinely shocked. People usually avoided me completely. They certainly didn't ask me to *dance*. The thought of Icarus pushed through my sudden elation. 'I'm sorry, Thom, I can't.'

'Oh, OK,' he said, looking down with a small smile. 'I'm not very good at dancing anyway,' he said.

'Me neither,' I told him and we both looked around the room awkwardly, the conversation now broken.

'Isn't that Tak?' Thom said suddenly, pointing. I turned and looked at the dance floor.

Tak was dancing to a slow song, the rhythmic beat pulsing through the room, his arms locked around the waist of a tall, pretty girl. It was Roz, I realized.

Oh no. Where was Zali? But before I could tear my eyes off the pair to look for her, Roz was leaning into him and their lips met.

'Good for him!' exclaimed Thom. 'Roz is alright.'

I hardly heard him, scanning the temple for Zali's dark curls, praying she hadn't seen the kiss. But when I finally found her, she was standing staring at Tak and Roz, a hollow expression on her face.

'I have to go,' I told Thom quickly. 'Thank you though, for talking to me.'

'Yeah, sure, any time,' he called after me as I raced towards my friend.

'Zali?'

She turned her face to me as I reached her, and I could see the tears in her eyes straight away. I glanced sideways at Tak and Roz, still on the dance floor and still kissing.

'I told you he didn't like me,' she whispered. I only just caught her words over the beat of the music.

'Zali, Roz kissed him, and you know what boys are like-' I started, but her lip started to wobble and then she was running past me. I jogged to the punch table, put both my glasses down, and took off after her towards the exit.

I found her in our room, crying quietly on her bed.

'Oh Zali, I'm sorry,' I said, sitting down gently beside her. She looked up at me, her tear streaked face making my heart ache for her.

'I knew it. I knew it all along,' she said sadly.

'Just because they got carried away and kissed at a dance doesn't mean he doesn't like you,' I said.

She scowled at me, fresh tears falling from her amber eyes.

'I think it's pretty clear who he likes,' she said.

'He may only be with her because he doesn't think you're interested.'

She shook her head.

'No. I can't compete with Roz. She's gorgeous and clever and funny and...' she trailed off.

'You're all those things, and more,' I told her, taking her hand and squeezing it. 'And you're his best friend. I'm sure if he knew how you felt-'

'No! No way am I ever telling him now,' she said fiercely. 'No, he's made his choice.'

'They just kissed. I don't think there was any choice-making involved,' I said gently.

Zali huffed.

'I don't care. I'm moving on. Like you said before, there are plenty of attractive demigods at this school to choose from.' She sat up straight as she spoke, swiping at her wet cheeks with her palms.

'Well, if you're sure, then good for you,' I said.

'I am sure. Tomorrow you're going to see a new Zali. One that's not waiting for an idiot boy to grow up.'

'Sounds awesome,' I told her, and leaned forward to give her the biggest hug I could.

15

I woke a number of times in the night though, dreams of swirling fire and raging tidal waves jerking me out of sleep, and I was sure I could hear the soft sounds of crying coming from Zali's side of the room. I wanted to go to her, to try to help, but I knew when I was sad I needed time alone. I prayed that she would start the next day feeling the feistiness I'd seen in her, instead of the hollowness I knew first-hand from losing Icarus's trust. When I thought about him, and the look on his face when Thom had come over, I couldn't help cringing. I knew that for once I hadn't done anything wrong, but the timing was awful. *Typical.* But I clung to the fact that he *had* been willing to talk to me. He had even brought me a drink. Surely that had been a peace offering? It opened the door to me trying to talk to him, at least.

. . .

I got out of bed before Zali the next morning and I left her sleeping as I went to breakfast ahead of my Sunday water lessons with Dasko. I figured she needed the rest.

'Are you doing anything to try and catch the death demon?' Dasko asked me as I stood in the shallow end of the pool, concentrating on holding a human sized ball of water above me.

'Of course I am,' I said, turning to him. The ball of water crashed down over me. I let out a long sigh as I peeled my wet hair from my face. This was why we were practicing in the pool, I reminded myself.

'Good,' he said. 'I wonder, if only a Titan could have let the demons out of that box then maybe only a Titan could destroy them.'

'Do you know how to destroy a death demon?' I asked him, a glimmer of hope in my words.

'There are a few ways, but they all require dangerous weapons or powerful beings. I think it's outrageous that the students are expected to deal with this themselves,' he said, his normally friendly eyes flashing angrily.

'So, the teachers aren't doing anything?' I asked, not expecting him to answer honestly.

'The teachers are doing what they can, but Zeus's orders were clear.' He looked at me, intense for a moment. 'What are you planning to do to kill it?'

I sighed, and started to speak, but I already knew what would happen.

'Professor Neos is the third demon. He's told me how

to make a potion that will lure the demon to us.' I watched as Dasko's face screwed up in frustration.

'That cursed language!' he exclaimed. Whenever I tried to tell him *anything* about Neos he couldn't understand a word I said.

'I'm sorry,' I said quietly.

'It's not your fault,' he sighed.

'It is.' My words barely came out a whisper and his stance softened as he looked at me.

'Pandora, most people would have opened the box. I don't blame you.'

'Icarus wouldn't have. He told me not to. *You* told me not to. And now those poor people are lying there with their souls stolen, all because of me.' Hot tears were gathering at the back of my eyes.

'Want to know a secret?' Dasko said.

I met his eyes and nodded.

'I knew you'd open the box.'

My mouth fell open.

'What?'

'If I'd had any idea at all of what was in it, then I never would have helped you find it, I swear,' he said, stepping towards me. 'But I knew that a Titan relic like that was sure to unlock both your powers. And I thought there would be more clues to where Oceanus and Prometheus are. I really had no idea at all that there would be dangerous demons in there. If anyone is to blame, it's me.' His earnest, honest eyes were locked on mine and something close to relief was washing through me. It was still my fault I'd opened the box. Nobody forced me to do that. But at least I could share the burden with someone else. At least I knew Dasko would have done the same thing.

'Why did you tell me not to open it?'

He spread his hands apologetically.

'I had to. It was the best way to ensure that you *did* open it. And if you hadn't, then we'd have given it to Zeus as planned.'

I stared at him, trying to work out how I felt. Had he used me? But to what end? Nothing in the box could have helped him, he wasn't a Titan.

'Why do you want to help Titans so much?' I asked him suspiciously.

'I told you before, I think it's time your ancestors and the Olympians made amends. Immense power could be unlocked if the immortals worked together. You're the key to that, Pandora. You and Icarus.'

'Icarus will be furious with you,' I said quietly.

'If you tell him, then yes, probably.'

'We're, um, not talking right now.'

Dasko quirked an eyebrow.

'You need each other. Especially if you want to defeat this Keres demon. You two are the strongest students in this school.'

I screwed my face up.

'That's not true.'

'Maybe not yet, but you have the potential to be.'

I looked at him doubtfully.

'What's in the ocean around us right now?' he asked me.

I pushed my consciousness out into the sea easily, barely having to concentrate to do it.

'The turtles are half a mile under us, there's a pod of dolphins to the east.... Three whales above us. And something else but it's not something I've seen before. Some sort of serpent I think,' I answered.

Dasko smiled at me.

'Do you know how rare it is to be able to do that?'

'But I can't even control the water in this pool properly.'

'That will come with time and practice. But your raw senses and power... that can not be taught, Pandora. And the way that Icarus can feel and manipulate air is the same. You two could achieve incredible things.' I thought about Icarus soaring through the skies over the glittering ocean and an overwhelming feeling of belonging built inside me.

'I have to get him to forgive me first,' I mumbled.

'What did you do?'

'I lied to him.'

'His upbringing wasn't like other kids. He may take longer to forgive than you would. But I'm sure he will. You two have a bond.'

A bond. I liked that. I hoped to the gods it was true. I missed his wicked grins, the way his eyes lit up when he talked about seeing the world, the gentleness behind the hard front he put on. I missed his kisses.

'I hope so,' I said.

But in flying class on Monday morning he walked straight past me, and looked at nobody the whole lesson. He leaped from the ledge as soon as Miss Alma said he could, and didn't return until the end of class. He still wasn't coming to sit with us at meal times either but to my dismay, Roz *was*. She and Tak made small playful faces at each other over their food, whilst Zali stabbed moodily at hers. She was putting on a brave face, trying to come across as indifferent, but I could see the sadness in her eyes when she looked at him. Tak didn't seem to notice that his best friend wasn't herself and I wondered how he could be so clueless. I wasn't so sure now that Zali had been wrong about him liking her. Maybe he really wasn't interested in her in a romantic way.

Much as wanted to dislike Roz, for the sake of my roommate, I couldn't. She was bold and funny and asked me questions about my life back home. I found myself caught up in her wide-eyed reaction when I told her about films and TV screens and the cinema.

'That sounds unbelievable,' she breathed.

'It *is* unbelievable. It's all made up, on computers and stuff,' I said. 'Not like here, where it's real.'

'So in a world where you can't see and mostly don't believe in magic, you make pretend magic for people to read about and watch?'

'Well, yeah,' I said.

'And you can make it look real, even though it isn't?'

'With actors and computers, yeah.'

'That's crazy,' she said.

I laughed.

'I guess it is. If I ever go back, I'll bring you back a movie.'

'Never mind that, I want one of those computer things,' she said.

16

On Tuesday I had Advanced Magical Objects class, and I entered the underground classroom to a weirdly tense hush. Suppressed murmurs rippled through the few other students as they crowded around the long table at the end of the room and I moved closer, curiously. My eyes fell on three goblets, all completely different from each other.

'Good day, class,' Professor Fantasma's voice croaked across us. Students stepped aside to let her ghostly form reach the table. 'As promised, we're going to look at cursed objects today.' I felt a surge of excitement. 'These three vessels can hold liquid. One will turn that liquid into precious metal. One will turn the liquid into a powerful seeing tonic. The other will kill the drinker.' I drew in a sharp breath. 'Who would like to guess which does what?'

Nobody stepped forward but everyone craned their necks, peering closely at the goblets. The first one was the largest. It had a rim of tiny blood-red rubies pressed into the bright gold metal it was made from. The ring of rubies was repeated halfway down the body of the goblet, then small strips ran down the length of the stem, fanning out at the bottom on the base of the cup. The second goblet was made from a shining silver metal. It didn't have any gems encrusting it, but it did have intricate, beautiful patterns carved all over it. I could see Greek columns, swirling clouds, curling vines and roses and much more. The last goblet seemed to be made of marble. It looked identical to the rock that made up the columns in the temples, thin veins of ash color running through the white material. It was shorter and stubbier than the other two and it looked heavy.

'Does the gold one make the precious metal?' asked a girl called Skye.

'What makes you think that?' Fantasma asked her.

She shrugged.

'It's gold and has expensive gems in it.'

'Very good. But no. It's meant to make you think that but it's a trick. It's actually the lethal one.'

'Then the silver one with the patterns is the seeing tonic one,' said a boy called Felix. 'Aren't the patterns something to do with oracle language?'

'Very good indeed,' Fantasma praised him. 'These are the glyphs the oracles used to curse objects with magic.'

My mind flashed on the suit of armor I'd seen the night we'd sneaked into the advanced tower, and the swirling patterns I'd seen appear on the leather fighting gear my reflection had been wearing. Surely that hadn't been anything to do with oracles?

'Why would seeing the future be a curse? Surely the goblet is a gift rather than a cursed object?' Skye said.

'To see one's own future is no gift, I assure you,' the professor said seriously.

If I knew my own future, I'd know if I would ever get back to dad and Mandy, I thought. I'd know if I was going to be able to catch the death demon and return the souls I'd caused to be stolen. Would that be worth seeing something bad?

'So, the last and most simple goblet creates precious metal. That marble cup is one of the most valuable things in all of Olympus.'

We all peered closer at it.

'How come it's here in the academy then, instead of with someone rich?'

'Aha, that's a very good question, Pandora,' Fantasma said. 'Line up here,' she said, and motioned for us to stand in front of the goblets. 'I want you all to hold each goblet for a moment or two. Close your eyes and *feel* for magic. Feel for the cup's desires, its strength and its needs. Try to work out if you trust each one.'

I waited nervously behind Felix as he held the gold cup. It had taken weeks for me to sense Nix in the phoenix feather, wouldn't these be the same? Felix moved on to the next goblet with a small shudder and I stepped up to the table. I studied the goblet a moment, the rubies a deeper red than I'd ever seen. They really did look like blood. I hesitantly put both hands on the goblet and lifted it. A cold tingle passed through my fingers as they made contact and I jumped slightly, my nerves on edge. I'd felt that feeling at home before, but always written it off as static shock. I concentrated, and the tingle changed. It was as though ice was filtering from my fingertips all the way up my arms. As I looked at the cup the red of the rubies seemed to blur and grow, as though the metal was turning that deep red too.

I put it down quickly, goosebumps raised everywhere across my skin.

'Evil. Definitely evil,' I muttered. The beautiful silver cup was next. I picked it up almost eagerly, turning it in my hands to inspect the intricate carving. There was no specific image, it was just as though somebody who loved flowing lines and tight spirals had doodled all over it, with a perfect result. I concentrated, trying to feel something from the goblet. But there was nothing. No hum or fizz or tingle of energy. No sense of hope, happiness or doom. Just... nothing. I shrugged and placed it back on the table, stepping up to where Felix had just returned the marble goblet. He gave me an uneasy look and I frowned as I picked it up.

I needed this goblet. *I needed this goblet.* The thought flooded my mind, repeating itself over and over again. Not just the goblet. I glanced around the room, searching for glinting metal or shining jewels. I needed all of it. All these precious things were wasted down here in this windowless pit! The thought was so strong it scared me, and I forced myself to drop the cup back on the table. I let go too early and it teetered alarmingly on it's base a moment, then mercifully settled flat.

'Are you alright, Pandora?' Professor Fantasma asked me.

'I, um, the goblet...' she smiled knowingly at me, then

motioned for me to sit with the others who had already handled all the goblets.

'So, class,' she said, when we were all sitting on the cushions on the floor. 'Who wants to tell me what they felt?'

'The gold cup is evil,' said a few people in unison. The professor nodded.

'It is an old curse that binds that one. Few would be foolish enough to drink from it now, when its evil is so ingrained with the metal that it seeps so clearly from it. But it wasn't always so. When the curse was fresh, the intent of the cup was still hidden, and many died as soon as their lips left the metal.'

'The marble cup made me feel... greedy,' said Felix, quietly.

'Me too!' I exclaimed. 'Like I wanted all the expensive things in the room.'

A few other students nodded but most looked interested.

'Indeed. That goblet belonged to King Midas. The curse on it would cause anybody who used it often to value wealth before anything else in the world. You would happily turn your whole family into gold, just to be surrounded by more treasure.'

I stared at her in horror. How could anything make you love gold more than your own family?

'That's why it is down here. Nobody is foolish enough to want unlimited wealth and eternal loneliness.'

I gaped at the goblet. I needed to be more careful with what I touched, I thought, not for the first time since my incident with the armor.

'When I touched the silver one, I felt really curious about my life and what I'm going to with it,' said Skye.

'Yes. That curse will make you burn with desire to discover truths about your future. But if you were to drink from it you would likely only see riddles that would confuse and haunt you for the rest of your life. Oracle sight is unreliable. What you see is not always unavoidable but can shape your every action forever. Nobody wants to live like that.'

'I didn't feel anything,' I said. Fantasma looked at me.

'Really?'

'I tried, but there was nothing.'

'How very, very interesting,' she said, peering over her glasses at me. 'Did everyone else feel curiosity about their future when they held the silver goblet?'

Everyone nodded, yeses ringing out around me.

'Pandora, stay for a few minutes after class please. This is very interesting indeed.'

My stomach squirmed. What did that mean?

We spent the rest of the lesson looking through textbooks for examples of cursed objects that gave off auras of power that helped identify what they did. At the end of the class I stayed sitting on the floor and watched everybody else leave apprehensively.

'Come here please, Pandora,' Fantasma called from the table. I got up and joined her leaning over the silver goblet and holding a tiny jug. 'There are only a few reasons you would feel nothing from the goblet. Either there's something about your Titan powers that negates it and stops it working, or you have such an undecided, turbulent future ahead that the cup can't fathom it.' I blinked.

'Hopefully the first,' I said quietly.

'Indeed. Look into the cup. Do you see anything?'

I leaned over to look into the bowl.

'You've filled it with water?' I said.

'Look harder,' she tutted, rolling her eyes. 'Place your hands on the base of the goblet.'

I did as she told me. At first there was nothing, exactly as before. But then I started to feel a slight heat coming from the metal. The water began to ripple slightly, then swirl around the shining cup. Then... Flames. There were *flames* in the water. I felt my mouth drop open. The flames were racing around, merging with the tiny whirlpool, fiercely orange in the clear liquid.

'There's fire in there,' I breathed.

'Fire? Oh dear,' said Fantasma. I looked at her and the heat under my fingertips died instantly.

'Oh dear?' I repeated. 'What does that mean?'

'It means that your Titan powers were not blocking the goblet's powers.'

I thought about that as she gently removed the cup from me, sliding it to the other end of the table.

'So I have a... turbulent future ahead of me?' I asked, remembering her words from moments before.

'It looks that way. Sorry dear.'

I groped for something to say as she began bustling about, tidying up the students' books.

'Is there anything I can do to make it... less turbulent?'

'I doubt it. I suppose it's not surprising though, what

with you and that boy being the first Titan students in years. Your future might be difficult to read because you may end up back in the mortal world.'

My breath hitched. Would I be back there as an outcast, never able to settle anywhere with anyone I loved? Or as a powerful member of Olympus, able to come and go as I pleased?

'And there's nothing I can do?' I asked her again. She straightened and gave me a soft look.

'Just make good decisions. Live by your morals. None of us can do more than that.' I nodded at her. Gods, I hoped I would make good decisions. That hadn't exactly been one of my strengths in life so far. 'Now, be off with you, I have things to attend to. Those rafes aren't going to grow themselves you know,' she chided, moving towards the door. I began to follow her, then her words forced their way through my reeling thoughts.

'Rafes?' I repeated, freezing mid-step.

'Rafes, yes. Do you have an interest in aquatic plants?' she said, glancing at me over her shoulder.

'Yes!' I half-squeaked. Professor Fantasma paused and turned to me.

'Really?'

'Yes,' I said, nodding vigorously, my heart starting to pound with excitement. 'Yes, I love everything about the water so I've been reading about Scorpio's plant-life. I like the fire rafes the best.'

'Oh, now there's a beautiful plant,' Fantasma said dreamily.

'Do we have any here, at the academy?' I asked, trying not to hold my breath as she screwed up her ghostly face.

'Oh no, dear, they only bloom for twelve hours.'

I felt my face fall as my excitement drained away instantly.

'I have plenty of seeds though.' I snapped my eyes to hers. 'Would you like some?'

17

I arrived at water class ten minutes late, but when I explained to Dasko that it was because Fantasma had held me back he gave me a nod and told me to go and practice at the water-wall. I went over to it quickly, my mind racing. I didn't know whether to try and tell Icarus about the seeds Fantasma had given me or not. And how would I plant the fire rafe? The plants needed to grow in a tank, somewhere secret so that nobody would ask questions or interfere with them. Nix's words flashed into my head.

'...that highly cultivated aqua garden underneath the school...'

That was it! I would plant them under the school. They would be safe there. And I could do that without Icarus's help, as long as the breathing bubbles turned up. The sooner I planted them, the better, I thought as an image of the attacked girl's black eyes filled my mind. I would sneak out and plant them that night, once everyone was asleep, I decided. Then I would have something good to tell Icarus when he was ready to talk to me.

My leg jiggled impatiently all through dinner, and I struggled to focus on what my friends were talking about. I was desperate for midnight to come around so that I could finally do something useful to help fix what I'd caused.

'Are you OK? You seemed really distracted tonight,' said Zali as we finally left the library for bed. She was still quiet herself and I missed her perky cheerfulness.

'Yeah, I'm fine. Just had a weird class today,' I said.

'Oh yeah?'

As we walked back to our dorm room I told her about the goblets, and Fantasma holding me back.

'Turbulent?' Zali repeated when I'd finished. She was frowning. 'That's a worrying way to describe someone's future.'

'That's what I thought,' I agreed.

'Well, maybe the cup or Fantasma were wrong. Or maybe turbulent is a good thing,' she said.

I smiled at her. That was more like the optimistic Zali I had come to love.

'Yes. Let's hope so.'

After I had said goodnight and pulled my curtain across, I changed as quietly as I could into my swimsuit, then pulled my hoodie and jeans back on and got into bed. I waited impatiently for Zali's breathing to slow, going over my plan in my head. When I was sure she was asleep I crept back out of my bed, eased the door open, and slipped out into the hall.

I darted between the shadows of the buildings, more wary than I used to be about slipping out to meet Icarus. The death demon was somewhere in the academy, and Neos had said soul snatching wasn't their only weapon. It couldn't hurt to be careful. When I reached the edge of the pool I ducked behind one of the ornate columns and slipped off my hoodie and jeans. A thrill of excitement and anticipation ran through me when I thought about the glowing garden under the school. I couldn't wait to see it again. I slipped my consciousness into the ocean around me, sensing for anything I should be worried about. I felt the turtle family, a little way below, and something I thought was similar to swordfish back home quite far out to the west. No sharks or sea monsters. Something touched my shoulder and I almost shrieked in surprise, coming back to myself with a jolt and whirling around on my butt.

'Dora, it's me!' hissed Zali. I let out a massive breath of relief as I leaped to my feet.

'Zali! What are you doing here?'

'I wanted to see what you were up to! I know you sneak out all the time but I figured that was to meet Icarus and you two aren't talking at the moment. I was worried you were doing something dangerous,' she whispered. Her eyes flicked down to my swimsuit. 'What *are* you doing?'

'It's a long story,' I said. 'And it *is* dangerous. You should go back to the dorm.'

She gave me a stern look and put her hands on her hips.

'No way. You need to give me more than that,' she demanded. I looked at her face, set and fierce.

'OK, fine, but not here.' I grabbed her arm and pulled her towards the changing rooms. We slipped inside and I called a tiny fireball to light the dark room.

'What's going on?' she asked me as I sat cross-legged on the tile floor with a sigh.

'You honestly don't want to know,' I said as she sat down opposite me.

'Yes, I do. Especially if it's dangerous.'

'But-' I started and she cut me off.

'Dora, I haven't asked you about where your powers and Icarus's wings came from last semester, or why Dasko takes such an interest in you two, or what happened just before the inspection. Because I figured you would tell me if you could and that you were safe with each other. But with you two not talking and a death demon loose in the school and you sneaking out by yourself... I'm not going to drop this. You're my best friend. And...' She took a deep breath and fixed her eyes on mine. 'I can be brave. I'm not useless. I can help you. I *want* to help you.'

My heart felt like it was swelling in my chest as I stared at her determined face. She was willing to help me? Without even knowing what was happening? Before I could stop myself, words tumbled from my lips.

'I made a terrible, terrible mistake last semester. Dasko helped us find a box that only Titan magic could find. And... and I opened the box when I wasn't supposed to.'

'A box?'

'Yes. And...' I dropped my eyes to my lap and gulped. 'I let the demon out,' I whispered. There was silence, and I couldn't bring myself to look at my friend. Shame overwhelmed me, and I felt my eyes fill with tears.

'I take it you didn't know there was a demon in the box when you opened it?' Zali said eventually.

'Of course not! I would never, ever have opened it if I'd known I would cause this!'

'Oh Dora, then it's not your fault!' Zali said, and put her hand over mine. A hot tear splashed from my face onto her dark skin.

'It is though,' I gulped. 'Those girls, lying there with those awful soulless eyes... It's because of me.'

'Lots of people make mistakes. It's how we fix them that is important,' she said. 'Did the box have something to do with your powers?'

'Yeah,' I nodded. 'And Icarus's wings. There was a vial in there and a note that said we had to drink it. And it gets worse. There... there were two more demons in the box.'

'Um, I don't know what just happened, but I have no idea what you just said, after 'Icarus's wings'. I have never heard that language before,' Zali said, frowning.

'Oh gods, this is what happens when I try to tell Dasko important things. It comes out in this stupid Titan language only Icarus understands. I don't even know how it happens.'

'That's quite cool. I wish I could speak a secret

language,' Zali said. 'What are you doing tonight? Is it something to do with stopping the demon?'

I looked at her.

'Yes. It's hard to explain, without the Titan language taking over, but I have a list of things I need to get that will help catch it. One of the things is a fire rafe.'

'What's that?'

'It's an aquatic plant, that takes four weeks to grow and only blooms for twelve hours. I managed to get some seeds from Fantasma today, and I need to plant them as soon as possible.'

'In the pool?' Zali looked confused.

'No. Last semester, when we were looking for the box, we found a secret underwater garden. Under the school.'

Zali's eyes widened as she stared at me.

'A secret underwater garden?'

'Yeah. It's upside-down, on the underside of the marble slab the academy is built on. And it glows.'

'That sounds like the coolest thing *ever*,' she breathed.

'It is pretty amazing,' I agreed.

'And that's where you're going now? How do you breathe?'

'Every time I've been before these little turquoise bubbles have wrapped around me and I could breathe fine. They wrapped around Icarus too. I guess they're part of the garden.'

'I can't believe you've never told me about this. It sounds awesome!' Zali's voice was filled with excitement.

'You don't hate me then? For what I've done to Alexsis and Demitra and Kiko?'

Her face softened as she squeezed my hand again.

'You didn't do anything on purpose. And you're trying to fix it. Of course I don't hate you.' She gave me a pointed look. 'Let me help you.'

'Really? Because it *would* be great to have some help.'

'Secret glowing water gardens? Just try and stop me!'

18

By the time we both slipped into the pool my shame had subsided, and determination to make things right had taken its place again. And I couldn't help being a little excited at showing Zali my underwater discovery. Why had I never confided in her before? She was so kind and understanding, and it felt so good to have someone to talk to after so long without my conversations with Icarus. I couldn't tell her everything, like about Neos or about Icarus's past, but it seemed I *could* tell her about the ingredients. Maybe she could help me with the manticore feather too?

'Ready?' she said, turning to me at the edge of the dome. Nodding, I took a big breath, and ducked under the water and pushed through the dome. I kicked hard, angling myself downwards and I saw Zali's legs shimmer out of existence as she powered past me, her shining, iridescent tail taking their place. I stayed close to the marble slab, relieved when we reached the bottom. I gripped the edge of the rock and Zali swam up beside me and did the same. Pulling hard, I flipped myself under the slab. The disorientating whirling began, tumbling me through the water over and over, and causing adrenaline to surge through my body. When I finally came to a stop I tipped my head up. The garden clung to the rock above me, hundreds of plants and fish pulsing with electric colors. My chest ached through my wonder though and I looked about for the breathing bubbles. A flash of turquoise caught my eye, then they were spiraling out of the depths towards me. I held my arms out happily and they curled about me until they reached my face. I closed my eyes and took a tiny, testing breath. Dry air filled my mouth so I took a bigger breath, relaxing. I looked around for Zali, and saw the bubbles surrounding her too. She was holding her arm up to her face, gaping at them, a goofy grin on her face. I pointed up and she leaned back, her jaw going slack as she took the garden in. Her amber eyes found mine again, alight with amazement and I smiled at her. I kicked up towards her and she fell in beside me as we swam along the coral, watching the fish dart in and out of the rocks and the swaying, shining plants. I looked carefully for anything that resembled fire rafes, just in case there were already some down there, but there was nothing like the picture I had seen. I hadn't thought I would be so lucky.

I kept swimming, looking for the area we had found the mushroom things that had lured the snake away from the cave. I remembered that they had been in some sort of soil, so maybe there would be space to plant the fire rafes near there. When I found the spot, I was relieved to see that there was definitely plenty of room in the dark, muddy looking soil. I rolled onto my back to face the little patch of red mushrooms above me, my power keeping me buoyant enough that I hardly needed to kick my feet to hover in place. I tentatively reached out towards the soil, and yanked my hand back as the purple shock shot through the water in front of me. Zali grabbed my shoulder and I rolled, looking at her alarmed face. Pushing my senses out into the water, I felt for something that might be causing the purple zap of energy. It was an eel, I realized. I couldn't see it amongst the reeds at the side of the mushroom patch, but it's presence kind of glowed and I could *feel* it there. I pointed, reaching out and rustling the reeds by their tips. There was a slither of movement, then suddenly the eel burst from the plants. I snatched my hands back as purple energy crackled around the creature, and little neon fish scattered around us. The eel was incredible to look at. It pulsed with the same electric light the rest of the garden did, a pale and intense pink. As it raced back and forth in front of the mushrooms, small bursts of lightning rippled down its serpentine body like veins, then shot into the water around it. It seemed it was taking its job of guarding the mushrooms very seriously.

Zali's grip on my shoulder tightened and I looked at her again. She was focusing hard on the eel, her amber eyes intense and alive, and her lips pinched tight. Was she trying to communicate with it? I looked back at the eel. It's frantic darting backward and forwards was slowing down and the pulses of electricity coming from it seemed to be lessening too. Slowly, it came to a complete stop, hovering in front of the patch of mushrooms, it's long body rippling in the water. Then its head snapped to face Zali, it's long jaw opening and closing a few times, before it darted off, wiggling past us in a harmless flash. Zali let go of my shoulder and she was beaming. I clapped, bubbles forming around my hands as they met. I definitely should have thought to bring Zali here before.

I dug into the soil a little, piling what I removed into Zali's cupped hands, then pulled the little bag I had tied around my neck open. There were four seeds and Fantasma said there was a good chance one or two of them would bloom. I buried the seeds in the thick plant bed, then packed the dirt from Zali's hands back in tight, so that they couldn't fall from the soil. After a thorough inspection of our handiwork, we kicked away from the mushroom patch and headed back towards the edge of the garden. We took our time, Zali marveling at the coral and rocks that teemed with sea-life. At one point she dragged me right up close to a rock so that I could see a slug-like creature with intricate orange and purple patterns all over its squishy body. I couldn't help keeping a wary eye out for huge sea snakes, even though I knew I didn't need to. My powers were aware of everything living in the garden and where they were at all times. The snake we had encountered before was just outside the cave, a massive presence. There was something as large on the other side of the garden, further than I had been before, and I thought it might be a giant crab. And there were lots of big fish, some flat and laying against the rocks, some the size of sharks, flitting in and out of plants. None of them were interested in us.

Eventually we reached the edge of the slab, and as I approached the swirling current that bordered the garden the turquoise bubbles began to uncoil themselves from my limbs. I said a grateful mental farewell, took a massive breath, and swam through the current, kicking hard. The academy pool came into view as my lungs were just starting to protest and I pushed through the dome and broke the surface happily. I had done it. No, *we* had done it. The fire rafes were planted. We were one step closer to helping catch the soul snatcher. Zali popped up beside me in the water, her eyes sparkling.

'Eeee!' she squeaked as she pushed her hair back from her face. 'I spoke to the eel! Not just the eel! I spoke to so many fish! That place... Dora, it's so incredible!'

'It's beautiful,' I agreed, smiling at her. 'Thank you so much. I couldn't have gotten the eel out of the way without you.'

'That's OK. I just asked it nicely,' she beamed.

'Of course you did,' I laughed.

I went to sleep that night hopeful for the first time since Icarus and I had broken into the advanced tower. Zali had enthusiastically volunteered to help check on the progress of the plants growth and now I had four weeks to find a manticore feather. And not flunk my exams and get kicked out of the academy.

Between my never-ending detentions with Neos, my extra classes with Dasko and the ramp up in assignments for all our classes, the next week flew by. I looked for Icarus every time we were in the temple or in a class together, but he avoided my eye so deliberately I couldn't bring myself to go and talk to him. It was so obvious he didn't want me to. Incredibly, Thom did though. He stopped me after breakfast one morning with an awkward wave.

'I, um, wondered if you'd learned everything you needed to about manticores yet?' he asked me, leaning against a column as we stood in the main temple.

'Oh, I'm sure there's always more to learn,' I said, smiling. I liked talking to him, even if I did feel slightly uneasy about Icarus when I did. He was nice, and genuinely friendly.

'Well, there are some really good books in the library. Maybe we could check some out together. Maybe tomorrow night?'

I faltered. Was he asking me on a date? The slight unease about Icarus exploded as my mind flashed on the hours Icarus and I had spent between the bookshelves over the last few months.

'Oh, I can't, I have detention. Sorry,' I said quickly, and darted off towards the temple exit before he could say anything else. I felt bad for running off, but my head had filled completely with green eyes and black wings and I didn't trust myself to talk to him any longer. I didn't know what I would say.

. . .

Tak and I had sword training later that morning and as we faced each other, wooden weapons in hand, he cocked his head at me.

'So, when are you and Icarus going to make up?' he asked.

I sighed.

'I can't force him to talk to me.'

'No, but you could try talking to him.'

'He clearly doesn't want to.'

'Attack!' Bellowed Agrius, and Tak lunged forwards with his sword, tapping me hard on the shoulder.

'No fair! You're distracting me!' I protested.

He shrugged with a grin.

'You'll be plenty distracted in a real battle. It's good practice.'

I lunged back, pretending to aim for his arm and dropping the sword and smacking into his exposed hip at the last minute.

'Ow!'

I grinned back at him.

'What about Thom then?'

'What about Thom?' I asked sharply.

'Well, he told me in last class that you blew him off.'

I said nothing, but parried the blow Tak aimed at my thigh.

'If you're not interested in Thom, and you're still into Icarus, go and sort it out!'

'It's not that simple. I wish it was.'

'Then you're over-complicating it.'

I glared at him, but part of me clung to his words. Was

he right? Was I making this worse than I needed to? Maybe Icarus *was* waiting for me to go and talk to him.

A clopping sound of hooves drew my attention and I saw Chiron approaching the training field. Slowly everyone stopped wielding their wooden swords and straightened as Agrius stomped over to meet the centaur.

'Vronti,' called Chiron when he reached us.

'Yes, headmaster,' the silver-haired boy said, stepping forwards. I noticed for the first time that he wasn't training with Astra. In fact, she wasn't in class. A chill rippled through me. 'Do you know where she is?' Vronti asked tightly, and I realized his skin was paler than usual. *Oh no.* I was getting a bad, bad feeling.

'Yes.' Vronti visibly sagged in relief at Chiron's response. 'But I'm afraid it's not good news.'

Vronti stiffened again, and he clenched his jaw, his face now white. The fear in his eyes sent stabs of anxiety jolting through my body.

'It got her, didn't it,' he whispered. It felt like ice was spreading through my body. No, please, *please* not the death demon. What about the potion?

Chiron dipped his head.

'I'm sorry,' he said.

A wail, unlike anything I had heard a human make, escaped Vronti. My impulse was to rush to him, but two students got there first, catching his elbows as he stumbled forwards, his head in his hands. An image of Mandy flashed into my head, and tears filled my eyes. I understood his pain. If anything happened to my little sister... I would be broken.

'Vronti, you need to tell me, why didn't she drink the potion?' Chiron said, with quiet urgency.

'We... we had a plan,' Vronti gasped. He wasn't crying, but his breathing was heavy and ragged.

'Have you drunk yours?' Chiron took a step towards him as he asked the question, as others stepped back nervously.

Vronti lifted his head and looked up at the centaur. Slowly, he shook it.

'No,' he whispered.

'Drink it now, fool boy!' roared Agrius, stamping forwards and grabbing Vronti's bag from the floor. He rummaged carelessly through it until he found a small bottle of the potion we were all drinking every morning. He thrust it at Vronti, who took it without looking at him. He wasn't looking at anything, his eyes glassy and his breathing now shallow.

'Drink it,' said Chiron, gently. Vronti unstoppered the bottle and tipped the liquid into his mouth without a word. 'Come with me,' the headmaster said, and everyone stepped aside as the centaur moved towards him, laying a hand on his shoulder and guiding him towards the temple.

Nobody made a sound long after they had disappeared from view. I felt sick. I thought I'd had time. I'd even started to feel hopeful, less guilty. I'd been an idiot. We weren't safe. Until the demon was stopped, nobody was safe.

19

Dinner that night was eerily quiet. The clack of knives and forks on plates was audible over the hum of nervous whisperings and my appetite was unusually absent.

'I hope Gida doesn't go through with his plan to lure the demon like that,' said Zali quietly.

'Me too,' I mumbled, looking around for the satyr. I spotted him, sitting with the older students he was always with when he wasn't with us.

'He's not stupid,' said Tak.

'Nor was Astra,' Roz said, giving him a look.

There was a pause.

'True.'

'Do you think it's coincidence that only girls have been taken?' Zali asked.

'I wondered that too. It does seem odd, four girls and no boys.'

I thought about that. Did death demons have a preference?

. . .

After dinner, in my nightly detention in the fire room, I decided to ask Neos.

'Why has the demon only taken girls?'

He sighed, and folded his arms across his chest, his red eyes flicking to mine. He kept them red the whole time we were alone together now.

'I don't know. It might just be coincidence.'

I raised an eyebrow.

'Really?'

Neos shrugged.

'There's no reason for her to only take girls. But both twins refused the potion and only Astra was taken. So there may be something we don't know.'

Great, I thought. That was just what we needed. More mysteries.

'But I wouldn't recommend the boys stop drinking the potion. Death demons are a tricky sort. Now, show me a fireball.'

I frowned, but conjured up a large fireball between us.

'Good. Now make it taller, and thinner.'

I did as he asked, making a column of fire almost as tall as I was.

'Now I want you to try something new. Put your hand in the flames.'

'What? No!' The fire in front of me died instantly.

'It won't hurt you. Not if you're truly connected to it.'

I considered that, trying to compare it to what I knew about my water powers.

'Then how come when I connect to the water, I can't breathe it? Isn't that the same thing?'

'You *can* breathe underwater, if you leave your body and *become* the water. I know that's how you defeated the sea demon.'

I stared at him.

'That's different. You're not asking me to leave my body, you're asking me to put my hand in fire.'

'And if you open yourself to the flames, they will not hurt you. Your magic will act as a barrier. Watch.'

He held up his arm, and tipped his head back. His eyes burned a brilliant scarlet, then suddenly his whole body was alight. I gasped, stumbling backward, but he tipped his head forwards again and laughed, holding his arms wide. Flames licked over them, dancing away from his body then leaping back again, every inch of him red and orange with fire.

'How...' I trailed off, staring.

'Only a fire demon, or a God, could do this Pandora. But you... You have Titan power in your veins. You have more potential than any student this school has seen for thousands of years.'

My breath caught. Was that true? Dasko had said something similar, though not such a bold claim. *Thousands* of years?

'You know, our detentions finished over a week ago.'

His words cut through my thoughts.

'What?'

'You didn't need to keep coming here after dinner. But you have anyway. You *know* the fire is within you. You need it as much as it needs you.' Flames leaped from his shoulders and he stepped towards me, his voice intense and seductive. 'Let it in. Embrace it. Use it. You could be incredible.'

He was right, I realized. About the detentions ending, about the fire. I could feel it inside me. I'd seen it in the suit of armor, I'd seen it in the goblet. *A turbulent future.* A future filled with fire, or water? Both, I thought, clenching my jaw in determination. I could control both, surely?

Tentatively, I opened my mind to the flames rolling across Neos's body. They rushed in and all at once I was more alive than I'd ever felt. Power and energy that was fierce and fast and erratic and desperate filled me. Neos held his hand out to me and before I could think, I took it.

There was heat, but it didn't burn. It tingled and fizzed, then surged, spreading through my body. I pulled my hand back slowly, holding it up and watching mesmerized as a solitary flame burned around my fingertips. I narrowed my eyes as the frantic feeling built, then, suddenly, fire was bursting from my hand. It flew down my arm and I screamed as it engulfed my chest, the heat now intense and real.

'Call the water!' shouted Neos. I squeezed my eyes shut, blocking out the roaring oranges and reds. I thought of the ocean around me, drawing as hard as I could on its strength and its power, its cool and solid presence. I gasped as cold water gushed from the water-wall, pouring over me like I was standing under a faucet and completely dousing the flames. I severed my connection with the water and it stopped just as abruptly as it had started. For a moment there was only the sound of water dripping from my clothes onto the stone floor and my ragged panting. Then Neos began to laugh.

'I've never seen anything like it!' His eyes were sparkling with excitement. 'Do you know how few people can work with water like that? To douse out fire *you* were controlling-'

I cut him off.

'I wasn't controlling the fire though! It's so frantic, so fast, I can't keep it where I want it.'

He waved his hand dismissively.

'That will come in time. Fire is a playful power, eventually you will learn its games.'

'I'm not sure I want to,' I said, my hands starting to shake. I wouldn't admit to him how scared I'd been as the flames had begun licking up towards my face. But I also wouldn't admit how I felt inside, holding those flames in my hand. Compared to water, fire was untrustworthy, but the feeling of life and freedom and building energy was... it was delicious. There was no better word I could think of to describe it. And the truth was, I wanted more.

My dreams that night, and all the following nights, were filled with giant tidal waves crashing against the beach back home, except it didn't look like it had the last time I saw it. Forks of crackling purple lightning tore across the ink black sky and the stones covering the shore were jagged and cruel looking. The monstrous waves hammering them over and over were lit by the eerie scarlet glow of flames that rippled and danced under the surface, impossibly beautiful and terrifying at the same time. I awoke from every dream with my heart pounding in my chest and sweat rolling down my face and back.

My struggle to control both water and fire not only plagued my dreams and my elemental classes, but it was also beginning to take its toll on my other studies. We were given practice tests in History of Mythology and Ancient Greek and I managed to fail both. I knew I shouldn't, but instead of revising for my written tests, I was still going to my nightly fire class with Neos. Every time I sat down with a book in the library with the others to try and learn the Greek words for animals, or the flying ship classes of Olympus, or the names of ancient river nymphs, burning energy swamped my body and I simply couldn't sit still. It was like the ocean around me was restless and the only way to calm it down was to use my power.

'Dora, do you want to help me revise for our practice geography test tomorrow?' Zali said pointedly to me at dinner a little over a week after Astra had been taken.

'Yeah sure, but I have to go to my fire class first,' I said around a mouthful of pasta.

'I think Neos would let you off the night before tests,' said Roz from across the table.

'Yeah, I mean, having elemental powers is kind of pointless if you get kicked out of the academy anyway,' added Tak. 'You'd have to go and live back in the mortal world, where you couldn't use them.'

I shrugged.

'I'll just cram before the actual tests. It's easier to learn stuff like that quickly. Elemental stuff takes time and practice.' I could hear Neos in my words, it was the same thing he and Dasko told me all the time.

'Hmm, well, the exams are only ten days away now. That is pretty close,' said Zali doubtfully.

'I'll be fine,' I told her.

But the geography test went so badly Chiron asked me to stay behind after class.

'Pandora, you got half of the questions on this test wrong,' he said gravely to me.

'I'm sorry,' I answered.

'It's not about being sorry, it's about making sure you learn enough to stay in the academy and become a productive member of Olympus. Is there anything wrong?'

I looked up at his warm, open, honest face that reminded me so much of my father's. *I let the death demon out, I have fire magic inside me that scares and thrills me, Fantasma says I have a turbulent future, I can't sleep and Icarus hates me.* I squashed my thoughts and said,

'I just know so little about Olympus, coming from the mortal world.'

Chiron frowned at me.

'That's no excuse, Pandora. Would you like extra classes? I'm sure Dasko would be happy to help and so would I.'

I snorted involuntarily and the centaur raised his eyebrows.

'Sorry. It's just, I'm having a lot of extra classes already.'

'In fire and water. Yes, I heard. You know, all the classes here at the academy are deemed integral to your survival once you leave the academy. That's why you must pass them to stay. You do understand how important they are, don't you?'

'Yes, of course.'

'For you, they are even more important. You have no family or place in this world currently. You will be starting from scratch when you leave here, meaning nothing in your arsenal could be more helpful than knowing everything you can about the geography of Olympus, how gods and demigods and demons live, and how to read and speak the language.'

I stared at him. I was so determined to be able to get back home, I hadn't considered what he was saying. I would be starting from scratch. If I graduated, I would be sent out into Olympus with nowhere to go and no clue how to live there.

'I see that you and Icarus are spending much less time together,' Chiron said gently. My stomach muscles clenched and I dropped my gaze.

'Yes,' I said quietly.

'You should try to patch that up. He is a very clever young man and you two achieved something truly great with that sea demon last semester. You can help each other.'

'Does he need help?' Concern filled me.

'Not with his written studies, no. But the more he withdraws back into himself, the more he loses his ambition. And Olympus could use his ambition. He could be exceptional. Like you.'

I sighed.

'Everyone keeps saying that. Dasko says I have to be better at water, Neos says fire, you say this, Fantasma's stupid goblet says my future's all messed up anyway and then there's the demon...' I trailed off. Chiron fixed me with a serious look. I waited for the suspicious questions, trying to think of lies to cover my slip up.

'You don't need to worry about the demon just now. The potion is keeping people safe. Let people help you with your studies.'

'Yes, headmaster.'

'Would you like extra classes?'

'No, thank you. Zali has offered to help. And... and maybe Icarus will help me with language.'

Chiron smiled at me.

'He's one of the best in the school at ancient Greek.'

I had to run to make my water class on time when I left the geography room. Chiron's words went round and round in my head as I stood at the back of the water class, absent-mindedly making approximations of butterflies soar from the water-wall and whiz around me in circles. My Sunday sessions in the pool with Dasko were working. As long as I was near water, my control was becoming second nature.

Chiron was right, I was realizing. As alluring and important as my elemental magic was, as *fire* was, understanding the world I had been sucked into was equally as vital. The thought of roaming Olympus alone, confused and hopeless, was just as awful as the thought of going back to the mortal world without my family. Would I really be starting from scratch? The painful thought of my mom popped into my head. She had said she might 'look me up' if I graduated. Where did she live? A pang of guilt jolted through me as I realized this was exactly what Chiron meant. If I had paid more attention and read the books I was supposed to then I would probably know where sea nymphs like my mother lived.

'Zali?' She was sitting cross-legged on her bed with a book in her lap when I entered our dorm room after water class.

'Uhuh?'

'Is that offer to help me revise still open?'

'Sure it is.'

'Thank you,' I said gratefully, dropping my bag on the bed. 'I really messed up the geography exam. I'm not going to do my water classes with Dasko on Sundays any more, and I'm going to cut down the fire classes.'

'We have ten days, that's plenty,' she smiled at me.

'Really?'

'Course. But we have to go and check on the fire rafes tonight.'

I nodded. We had agreed to check on the plants weekly, so that if they weren't growing or anything happened, we could try and get more seeds as soon as possible. Although Zali was so enamored with the garden I thought she'd check on them daily if she could. They had been doing well last time we looked, the green shoots a good couple of inches out of the soil.

'Right. We can get in half an hour before dinner. Have you got your god lineage book?' Zali asked me.

'Yeah, somewhere,' I said, and started to hunt for the heavy book. 'I, um, thought I might ask Icarus to help me with language,' I mumbled as I bent over the pile of books at the end of my bed. I jumped as Zali squealed behind me, clapping her hands together.

'About time,' she beamed as I turned to her.

20

I clenched my sweating palms for the hundredth time, took a deep breath, and forced myself to step between the bookshelves. I could see Icarus, sitting on the floor with his tattered Sherlock Holmes book, his wings wrapped forwards so that he could lean back on the shelves. Heart hammering, I opened my mouth.

'Hi,' I said. He looked up at me and lowered his book. 'Hello.'

'Can I, um, join you a minute?'

His piercing green eyes bore into mine and my breathing quickened. I didn't need to be this nervous, I told myself sternly. I'd spent hours with this boy. He knew me and I knew him. *We had a bond.*

'I guess,' he said. That wasn't a good start.

I slid down the selves opposite him.

'I wanted to ask you a favor,' I said, figuring that getting to the point would be less awkward than small talk.

He raised his eyebrows.

'I'm failing Ancient Language. Chiron suggested that as you were so good at it you might be able to help me revise.'

'You're failing all your written classes, aren't you?'

I scowled.

'How'd you know that?'

'I'm not stupid. And you're spending all your spare time with that demon.'

There was an edge to his voice that instantly set me on the defensive.

'Are you spying on me?'

'No. But I've been keeping a close eye on Neos. And you're always with him.'

I stared at Icarus and he stared right back.

'He's helping me control my fire magic,' I said through gritted teeth.

'Sure. And you think it's a good idea to spend that much time with a demon that was locked away for eternity by a Titan?'

'If Oceanus had meant to lock them away for eternity he wouldn't have left a trail of clues to follow and a vial in there for Titan descendants to drink. He obviously meant for the box to be opened at some point,' I snapped.

'So now you're defending him?'

'No! But he's made some good points, and he's the only hope I have for stopping the soul snatcher. Plus I'm getting a lot better at fire.'

Icarus's eyes flashed and his wings fluttered around him.

'I don't trust him,' he snarled.

'*You* don't have to.'

'Oh really? So you're doing this all alone now?'

'I've not had much choice!' I regretted shouting it as soon as the words left my mouth. Icarus dropped my angry gaze and neither of us said anything for a long, long moment.

'I'll help you with language,' he said eventually.

'Oh. Thank you,' I said, surprised.

'But if you continue to trust that demon, I can't help you with anything else.'

Disappointment and annoyance thrummed through me. I hadn't come to him to ask for help with the potion or the demon, but he was the only person who knew the truth. How could he not see that Neos was our only hope?

'I don't have a choice, Icarus. If he'd wanted to hurt anyone, he's had months to try.'

'I don't think he wants to hurt you. I think he wants to use you.'

'For what?'

'I don't know.'

'Well, do you have any other suggestions to stop the death demon and get those poor girl's souls back?' I challenged him.

'Not yet. No.'

'Then I have to try.'

'Fine.'

'Fine.'

I got to my feet, anger pumping through me now.

'I'm doing my best, you know,' I said. 'To fix this.'

Icarus looked up at me and I saw a glimmer of the

real him that I'd come to know so well at the top of the pegasus tower.

'I'll meet you here for an hour after dinner for language revision,' he said.

I locked my eyes on his, willing him to say more. To tell me that he forgave me, or that he missed me. But he said nothing, so I turned and left, before my emotions could get the better of me.

He did meet me every day after that, but we spoke about nothing but ancient Greek. Each time I found myself watching his lips as he spoke, or wishing his hand would brush mine as we sat over a book, I recalled his words. *If you continue to trust that demon, I can't help you.* The memory riled me enough every time to push the soppy thoughts from my head and concentrate. If he would rather I left my fire magic untamed and uncontrollable and faced the death demon alone, then so be it. I didn't need him. There was no doubt he was improving my language skills though. He had a weird little technique that made it infinitely easier to remember the complicated words. He would make me think of something similar to the word we were learning, then visualize it with the meaning. So the Greek word *skafos* reminded me of the word *scaffolding*. Icarus didn't know what scaffolding was, but that didn't matter. What mattered was that *skafos* meant 'boat', so when I pictured a boat all covered in scaffolding, it was easy to remember.

Zali was testing me every morning and every night on the god's powers and family trees, and in the library in the evenings Gida was testing all of us on the twelve realms of Olympus. Roz was almost as bad at geography as I was, so he gave us both the most questions. She had grown up on Cancer, Hera's realm, and apparently her family had little interest in the rest of their world.

Slowly, but surely, the exams crept closer but just as slowly and surely, I was feeling more prepared. I was squashing down the constant nagging reminder that I was still no closer to finding a manticore feather, but our third check on the fire rafe went well. The shoots were now two feet long, and something was beginning to bulge under the green skin of the long reedy plants. Nobody else had been taken since Astra and it seemed unlikely that anyone would risk not drinking the potion after what had happened to her.

When the morning of the first exam rolled around I was awake early, and feeling as ready as I ever would. They were spaced out over three days, ten of them in total and first up was flying. There had been speculation that an obstacle course of some sort would make up the test, and when we reached the top of the pegasus tower, Zali and I saw that the rumors had been right. There were flaming rings hovering all around the tower, high and low, large and small.

'Hello class,' called Miss Alma as we all gathered on the ledge. 'Hermes will be joining us momentarily to oversee the exam. There is no race today, you will take your turns one-by-one. You need ten points to pass the exam, and you will get a point for each of the fourteen rings you fly through, except for the highest and lowest rings, which are worth two points. You will have three minutes each. Please saddle your pegasi.' I wished Zali luck, did my best to catch Icarus's eye but failed, and jogged to Peto's stable. He was as restless as I was clearly able to feel the nervous energy buzzing through the students now noisily clattering around the stables.

'We're going to ace today,' I told him as I heaved his saddle on his back. He snorted. 'I'm going to let you be in charge. Just fly through as many rings as you can.' When the pegasus was ready to go I led him carefully from the stable and back to the ledge, where a few students were already waiting. There was a burst of bright white light, then Hermes was standing next to Miss Alma. She bowed her head low and I followed suit along with the others.

'I haven't ridden a pegasus in years,' the god said cheerfully. I blinked. 'Can I have a go, after the kids are finished?' He looked expectantly at Miss Alma.

'Of course, Lord Hermes,' she spluttered.

'Excellent,' he beamed.

Icarus went first. I watched, enthralled, as his huge wings snapped taught behind him and he dove from the ledge. I wasn't the only one to lean forward over the edge of the platform to watch as he tucked his wings around him and shot towards the lowest flaming ring like a dart. As he got closer he spread his wings wide, turning sharply and angling himself towards the hoop, then tucking them around himself again as he zoomed through it. I hardly breathed as I watched him, soaring around the course like it was the most easy, natural thing in the world. We had flying class together twice a week but he always took off around the tower, flying well away from everyone else. He'd clearly been practicing hard. As he landed back on the platform with all fourteen rings cleared and a full three seconds left on the clock, everyone burst into applause. His cheeks colored pink and I was nearly overwhelmed by the urge to go to him.

'Well. I've not seen anyone fly like that in a while. Well done,' said Hermes. This time Icarus's whole face went red and he shook his windswept hair over his face as he bowed his head.

'Thank you, Lord Hermes,' he mumbled.

'Next!' called Miss Alma.

I was fifth to go and Peto was desperate to get off the platform by the time I climbed up into the saddle and locked my red Converse into place. It was like he was getting jealous watching everyone else having all the fun.

'Ready boy?' I whispered to him, scratching behind his ears. He shook his enormous wings out hard and whinnied.

'Let's go!'

He flew like a dream, banking hard but accurately as we approached each burning hoop and tucking his wings in just enough as we flew through the sudden heat. The fire felt different each time we got close to a ring, like it was calling to me. I concentrated on the churning waves below me, trying to block the feeling out and draw stability from the ocean. But as we flew towards the ninth ring, my vision blurred slightly. I screwed my eyes shut, trusting Peto, and when I opened them I screamed. The ring just feet in front of us was an inferno. Flames as big as the pegasus leaped and danced around it and Peto neighed loudly, beating his huge wings as he tried to change direction, but it was too late. We were too close, and his momentum was too great. I lifted one hand high in the air and called the water, praying it would reach in time as we barreled towards the flames. A solid jet of salt water rocketed up from the sea below, smashing into the burning ring and knocking it from our path with less than a second to spare. Peto wheeled up, and I could feel his legs kicking hard beneath me as we rose, away from the now spinning hoop.

'It's OK, it's OK boy. We're OK,' I tried to soothe him, my mind racing. Had I caused the flames to do that? I heard a gong sound and my attention refocused sharply. That meant I had ten seconds left. And I had only achieved eight rings. Adrenaline pumped through me. I couldn't fail this class, it was one of the few I was good at. There wasn't time to fly through two more rings, but the pegasus's efforts to avoid the last ring had taken us high above the main course. My eyes fell on the highest ring, now just a few feet above us. It was worth two points. 'Come on Peto, we can still do this!' I urged him up, and he responded, beating his wings fast. I clung to the presence of the water, refusing to even acknowledge the flames flickering around the ring. I channeled the heavy solidity of the ocean below, pushing all thoughts of fire out of my mind, and Peto tucked his wings in as we passed through the ring barely a second before the final gong sounded.

21

'Are you alright?' said Zali as we landed back on the platform. 'What happened with the fire around that ring? Gods, that was close.' She continued to fuss and ask questions as I climbed down from Peto's back.

'I'm fine,' I told her as I turned, then froze. Hermes was standing behind her, staring at me. Zali turned to see what had caused my wide-eyed look, squeaked and ducked to the side, bowing her head. I dipped my head too, heart pounding.

'Interesting,' the god said eventually. 'Next!'

None of the rings suddenly became lethal blazes for any other students and unease filled me as I watched them take their turns. Had *I* made the flames do that? I didn't think I had, but who here who could or would try to do that to me? I instinctively looked about for silver hair, mysteriously present whenever bad things happened to me at this school, but Vronti wasn't in my flying class.

Zali was last to go, and she did great, managing eleven hoops with no problem. Everyone in the class passed and Miss Alma looked pleased as we all trooped to the hauler.

'Which one is most fun to ride?' I heard Hermes ask her as we started to descend.

The next exam was archery, another one I was reasonably confident in. There was no Hermes to oversee this one, just Chiron and Agrius. As I'd hoped, I hit every target well, and ended up coming in the top five. And to my delight, I beat Tak by one place.

'I'll get you in swords!' he called playfully to me. I believed him.

Language was next, and my heart was skittering in my chest as we filed into the classroom. The flame dish in the middle of the room roared to life as we sat down, an image of a horse floating above it.

'This is a simple test,' said Dasko once we'd all taken our places. There was a numbered sheet of paper in front of us with lots of tiny line drawings next to a blank space. 'You just need to write the ancient Greek word for each image that appears in the dish. There is a drawing on your exam sheet to help you if you miss one. You have forty minutes.' I took a deep breath, and put my pen to paper as he called, 'Begin!'

Icarus's lessons paid off. When the forty minutes was

up, there were only four or five that I knew I'd got wrong and another couple that I'd made a half-decent guess at. But the rest, I had known. I tried to catch his eye again as we left the classroom but he looked resolutely ahead, ignoring everyone. A pang of sadness jolted through me as I realized I would have no excuse at all to sit with him each day now that the language exam was done.

My last exam that day was water element. Hermes was back, overseeing, but I felt no nerves at all as we lined up down the side of the room. When it was my turn, I tuned into the ocean surrounding the academy, and let its power fill me. I turned to the water-wall and held up my hands, remembering what Dasko had done the first day he had brought me into the water room. I drew the water above me, forming and shaping it with my will, until a small family of turtles made entirely from water swam through the air around my head. I smiled at the little gasps from my fellow classmates.

'Very good, Pandora,' said Dasko, beaming.

'Very good, indeed,' echoed Hermes, his voice ringing and lyrical. I glanced at the god, and lost control of the biggest turtle, taking a sharp breath as the cold water dropped from the air above me straight down my shirt. A few people laughed and Dasko chuckled.

'I still think that warrants a pass. Next.'

There was an air of exhaustion at dinner that night, and the temple nearly emptied once the plates and tables had vanished. Zali and I followed suit, and mercifully, I slept well for a change.

The first exam the next morning was History of Mythology. Zali and I tested each other on everything we had been revising all through breakfast, but my nerves still skittered as I took my seat in the classroom.

'You will have three tests. One on the Olympians, one on the Titans, and one on demigod demons,' Dasko told us all. 'Half an hour for each. You can turn over your first paper now.'

It went as well as I could have hoped. There were lots of questions I did know the answer to, like 'What is Nyx goddess of and who is her husband' and lots of questions I had to guess at, like 'How many children did they have and name three.' I thought I did best on the Titan questions, but I supposed it was unsurprising that I would remember the most details about my own ancestors. Dasko told us he would be marking all our written papers over the next few days, and we would have to wait for the results. We were given a twenty minute break until the next exam, which for me was Swords and Spears.

'Ready to get whooped?' Tak winked at me as I met him at the side of the training ground.

'Big words from a little boy,' I teased back.

'Oooh, you're on.'

'Class!' roared Agrius and we all fell silent. 'Today Hermes will be judging whether or not you are good enough to pass this test.' I gulped and Tak looked sideways at me. His face echoed my thoughts. *Maybe* we should be taking this more seriously. 'Choose either sword or spear. Swords over here, spears over there,' he bellowed, gesturing to either side of the field. It was an easy choice for me, I was much better with a sword than a spear. Tak looked at both sides thoughtfully for a moment, then shrugged at me and headed over to the spears. Gutted as I was to see my training partner leave, I thought he'd made the right decision. Tak was really good with a spear. Eight of us had picked swords and I looked around at the others, my confidence faltering slightly as I laid eyes on Vronti, standing straight and looking fierce and cold. Agrius stamped over to us and there was a now familiar flash of bright light, then Hermes was standing next to him. He ran his finger and thumb down his red beard as he regarded us all bowing our heads.

'Vronti, as head boy you can start. Pick your partner.' I seethed inwardly at Agrius's blatant favoritism, knowing exactly what would happen next. He did it every class and I never did well out of it. Agrius hated me.

'Pandora,' said Vronti, turning to face me. I made an effort not to groan out loud as adrenaline pulsed through me. This was going to be tough.

I took a wooden practice sword from the tub and Vronti and I faced each other in the center of the training ring. Part of me wanted to ask after his sister, but as I looked at his steely, emotionless face I couldn't bring myself to. What if he thought it was a cheap shot to distract him? Besides, I knew her condition wouldn't have changed.

'Three, two, one, go!' Agrius had barely finished yelling when Vronti came at me, fast and hard. I yelped as his sword crashed down on my shoulder, leaping sideways. *Pay attention, Pandora,* I chided myself. I focused in on his sword, his arms, tried to watch his muscles to anticipate which way he was going to move next. I parried his next three blows and managed to get one of my own in, which he easily blocked.

'Titans don't belong in this school,' he hissed at me as I panted opposite him.

I glared at him. He was wrong. I did belong here.

'I'm not dangerous,' I said, swinging at his legs. He jumped lightly out of the way and brought his sword down quickly at the same time, almost catching my wrist.

'Not with a sword, clearly,' he sneered. Anger spiked in me.

'Why do you hate Titans?' I asked him, lunging again and changing direction at the last minute. He moved fast but I just clipped his ribs.

'Zeus hates Titans, and there is no greater example to follow,' he said, glowering.

I pulled a face, adrenaline surging through me now as my anger built.

'What if I'm nothing like other Titans? How can you judge me knowing nothing about me?'

'My father says you are.'

My eyebrows leaped up in surprise. Zeus had said that? About me? The distraction was all he needed. Vronti charged forwards, bringing his sword down and kicking out at my legs at the same time. I threw myself into a roll, hitting the floor hard but avoiding both his sword and kick. I launched myself back to my feet as I came out of my tumble and blindly swiped the sword around me in an arc, hating that my back was to him. I felt a satisfying thud as my sword connected with something solid and I whirled around. Vronti was stumbling backward, a small trickle of blood running down the side of his face. Somehow, I'd hit him in the head.

'Enough! First blood to Pandora,' growled Agrius. 'Which is the only thing saving you because Vronti was clearly the better swordsman,' he glared at me.

'Agreed,' said Hermes. 'Next.'

Vronti gave a snarl of frustration, throwing his sword back with the others and stalking back to the group. He swiped at the blood on his brow and gave me a look that I was sure could wither plants, it was so full of venom. True hatred glinted in his eyes. I looked away uneasily and dropped my own sword back into the tub, panting slightly. I'd been lucky, but I'd passed.

My next exam was Magical Objects. When we entered the underground room the long table held three daggers. Professor Fantasma handed us all a sheet of paper and told us to go and sit on the cushions. Once I was sitting, I studied the paper. There was a simple sketch of each dagger and underneath there were three separate sentences. I read them carefully.

'This man is a fearsome hero, wise in battle and strong in might.'

'This man is a coward, who lies and cheats to save himself.'

'This man has no physical strength but would die to save his family.'

'Class,' said Fantasma, and we all looked up at her. 'You have five minutes with each weapon. I want you to match the weapon to its previous owner, as described on your paper. These were all very passionate characters, who have left strong imprints on their daggers. You should be able to work out who owned which.' I lined up with the others to take my turn holding the daggers, not knowing what to expect. It had taken me weeks to connect with Nix, but two of the goblets had given hints about their unpleasant intentions in seconds.

As soon as I picked up the first dagger I felt an overwhelming urge to hide amongst the bookshelves at the back of the room. I actually took two steps towards them before realizing what I was doing. Focus, I told myself. I concentrated on the weapon. It was a plain blade, with a worn handle wrapped in dark red leather. Did it want me to run because it was scared or because it wanted me to defend someone? I closed my eyes, trying to connect with it. A frisson of fear ran through me. This was the coward's knife, I was sure. The next dagger was delicate and feminine, and the hilt had three tiny rubies pressed into each side. I felt nothing at first, but after a minute or so, I couldn't keep dad and Mandy's faces from my mind. Was this the dagger of the man who cared so deeply for his family? When I took the last knife I was sure of it. The urge to use the dagger was huge. I wanted to use my arms, my legs, my power, I wanted to exert myself. There was no doubt this dagger had belonged to a fighter.

I went back to my paper and wrote down my answers. Most of the other students completed their papers in a similar time, but a couple kept returning to the knives, clutching them with eyes squeezed shut. When everyone had finally written something down, Fantasma collected the papers and told us we would get the results soon. It was probably the easiest and definitely the shortest exam I'd had so far, I thought as I headed back to my dorm room to start revising for tomorrow's geography test.

22

I was feeling nervous as I ate my breakfast on the third and final day of exams. Geography would be hard, but fire was my biggest concern. My patchy control over the volatile element made it impossible for me to feel confident about using it under pressure. At least swimming shouldn't be as bad.

Fire was my first exam of the day and I was restless when I reached the fire room, keen to get it over and done with. Hermes was already there when I entered, and I couldn't help noticing that Neos was keeping his distance. How was he hiding his identity from an Olympian? I thought of Icarus's words. *I don't trust him.* I had no doubt that Neos was more powerful than he was letting on. But as long as he could help with the death demon and my fire magic, I was sure I had no choice but to work with him.

There were only six of us in the class, so my turn came around quickly.

'Could you conjure a flame, please?' asked Neos as I

stepped up to the central dish. I summoned a small fire-ball, which hovered over the bowl. 'Thank you. Now, can you move it around?' I did as he asked. I prayed silently that he wasn't going to show Hermes what I could really do. If I lost control in front of Hermes I would fail. 'Good. Now extinguish it.' I snuffed the flame out. 'Now create a wall of fire at the end of the room.' I'd watched the previous three students go through the exact same motions, so I had no trouble doing everything he asked. Hermes nodded wordlessly when I finished and then the next student stepped up. As she repeated the steps, a sense of relief washed through me. I'd made it through the fire exam without setting anyone, including myself, on fire.

Geography was nowhere near as bad as I thought it would be. My hours and hours of revising with Zali and pop quizzes with Gida must have worked, because I actually felt a little excited when I saw the first of the three papers were on Olympian Ships. 'Describe the differences between Whirlwind class ships and Typhoon class ships.' I wrote fast, pouring everything I knew about the differences in the number of masts, types of weaponry and class of longboat each of the ships had. The second question was easy. 'Name the four forbidden realms.' Hephaestus' Scorpio, Hades' Virgo, Aphrodites' Pisces and Artemis' Sagittarius. 'Describe the seasonal climates on three realms of your choice.' I wrote furiously, citing the extreme seasons on Apollo's Capricorn, and the wild electrical storms on Zeus's Leo and the ever mild warmth of Hera's Cancer. When the gong signaled the end of the test I felt surprisingly pleased with myself.

The very last exam was swimming and I didn't feel as confident as I had expected to as I changed into my swim-suit. Arketa was so good at ruining my swimming classes, and had managed to beat me in almost every race one way or another. When we arrived at the pool I was relieved to find that Hermes wasn't present. Miss Alma was already in the water though and she beckoned us all in to join her.

'As with your other exams, this is not a race, but you have a time limit of eight minutes. There are five chests out at various points in the ocean. Some are only acces-sible through pipes and they all contain flags of different colors. You need to collect one of each color. There are two breathing boxes at the furthest edges of the course in case you can't get back to the pool.'

We had used breathing boxes in our classes before and I looked out at the ocean to try to locate them. They were small glass cubes filled with air that you could swim underneath and put your head in, and I could see one at each end of a massive network of pipes, bending up and down and left and right like a maze. I could also see two chests floating in isolation, one much further out than the other.

'You will go in groups of three. Arketa, Pandora and Alexander, you're up first,' Miss Alma said. My heart sank. *Of course* I would be in Arketa's group. I couldn't help looking at her as we waded through the pool towards the teacher. She gave me a spiteful glare in return. I would just avoid her, I thought. Go for whichever chest she *wasn't* going for.

'On my mark, get set, go!'

I launched myself from the pool through the dome with a big breath. Arketa went straight for one of the chests out in the open, and Alexander went for the other one. That left the maze of pipes for me. I swam quickly towards the closest entrance, my heart skipping a little as I saw how dark it was inside the navy blue tubes. I pushed my senses out into the water, hoping to find the chests inside that way, but I could only sense living things and the chests stayed invisible to my powers. I picked a direction and swam, my power creating currents to speed me up. The tubes gave off a kind of glow and it actually wasn't as dark as I had initially thought it was. They were wide too, and there were lots of short pipes leading off each one straight back out into the ocean so it wasn't claustrophobic. It only took a few seconds to find the first chest, sitting in the middle of one of the longer pipes, and I lifted the lid quickly, pulling out a yellow flag and tucking into the side of my swimsuit. I needed more air. I kicked towards one of the exits and emerged from the pipes on the left side of the course, and swam fast to the breathing box there.

I took a few big breaths as soon as my head was inside the dry box, looking through the clear glass for the other two. Arketa was at the second exposed chest and Alexander was nowhere to be seen. I ducked out of the breathing box and headed back to the pipes. Arketa would be going there next and I'd rather not come across here inside the tubes. I weaved through them, looking for the other two chests, pumping my fist when I finally came across the second one. I took the blue flag and swam towards another exit, clear blue water visible at the end of the pipe. Once I'd made a brief stop at the breathing box I dove back towards the pipes, passing Alexander on his way to get more air. He had a blue and green flag tucked in his shorts, so he still had the yellow chest to find in the pipes. There was no sign of Arketa. I headed as far to the right of the course as I could, then ducked into the pipes again, coming across the last chest almost instantly. I grinned as I pulled out the green flag and tucked it in with the others. Just the two easy ones left to get, I thought, as I span towards an exit tube. I went straight for the breathing box, hoping to get enough air to get the last two flags in one go, then get back to pool. As my head entered the air filled box I saw Arketa, pushing her head up into the other breathing box. I could just make out four colored flags at her hip and I screwed my face up. She was going to beat me. Again. Then my attention snapped to a movement behind her, dark and distant in the sea. I pushed my senses out quickly, probing the water for life, and recoiling as they hit the creature approaching the course. It was a shark. And it was hungry.

I waved frantically at Arketa, pointing behind her. At first she just glared at me, but then she turned. The shark was closer to her, and approaching fast. I took a massive breath and pushed myself down and out of the breathing box at the same time Arketa did but the shark was faster than both of us. My blood seemed to freeze in my veins as

I saw it gliding through the water towards her, it's jet black eyes shining and its mouth filled with razor sharp teeth. She was heading for the safety of the pipes, which were closer to her than the pool. The shark opened it's huge jaws and chomped down on empty water as Arketa slipped inside the pipe just as it reached her. Relief washed over me and I started to swim for the safety of the pool when I noticed Alexander pop out of a tube just a couple of feet from the shark. I felt its reaction, frustration turning to predatory calm as it locked onto the boy. I summoned my power, drawing as much as I could, then unleashed it at the shark, trying desperately to guide the burst of energy. I watched the tight current of water I had created slam into the shark, knocking it off course and out of the way of Alexander. His fear-filled eyes met mine and he swam faster than I'd ever seen him swim, towards me and the pool. My lungs were starting to burn, but Arketa was still in the pipes. I couldn't leave her there. The shark had wheeled, and its cold beady eyes found mine. With a flick of its tail, it began to speed towards me. I flung more energy out towards it, fear battering against my control as the creature opened its mouth, giving me a terrifying view of the teeth that would shred me to bits if I couldn't stop it. I could feel its excitement for the imminent kill. I closed my eyes, and poured my consciousness into the water around me. My vision changed completely, and the shark became a tiny blip in an infinite world of blue. I focused in on it, and pushed, with all the strength of the mighty ocean. I came back to myself and opened my eyes in time to see the shark flying backward through the water, so far it that it was soon indistinguishable in the distance. It was as though it had been flicked away like a fly. A spasm clutched my chest and panic bolted through me as my mouth opened involuntarily and sea water gushed in. Then strong hands were on my shoulders and I tried desperately to stop my body taking the breath it was desperate for as I was dragged, lightning fast through the water. We crossed into the pool but not before my lungs won. Pool water filled my mouth, nose, chest, and I was only dimly aware that I was being pulled out of the water and held up on my hands and knees. Blind panic had fully taken control of me and I couldn't breathe at all, until something hit me hard on the back, between my shoulders. I heaved, the water leaving my chest as retched over the tiles, and began taking ragged gulps of air.

'Slow down, slow down,' I heard a female voice say. 'You're OK.' It was Miss Alma, I realized. Spots were dancing in front of my eyes and I had a vile taste in my mouth.

'Arketa?' I gasped.

'I got her too.' I turned my head to see Zali next to me in the pool, tears pouring down her cheeks. 'I thought I was too late to save you,' she whispered. I didn't have the strength to answer her, but tried to give her a smile. I could hear someone else retching, and the strong hands left my back and I collapsed onto the tiles.

23

I was taken to the infirmary where Fantasma checked me over, and announced that I needed to be watched for a few hours. I felt sick, and shaky, and tired. Miss Alma came in half an hour later, supporting Arketa on her arm. She didn't say a word to me as she was helped into one of the other beds.

'I just wanted to let you both know, it was obvious you would both have collected all of the flags, so given the circumstances, you both passed the exam,' Miss Alma said gently. 'And Pandora, you did exceptionally well. You probably saved both of their lives.' Arketa looked up at me, her usual poisonous expression absent. She was frowning. 'Now, get some rest,' the teacher said and left the room.

'Why did you save me? You could have just let the shark eat me and not risked your own life,' Arketa said as the door swung shut.

I gaped at her.

'Are you serious? You think I'd leave someone to get eaten by a shark?'

She shrugged.

'Do you hate me that much?' I asked quietly.

'I know what your kind are capable of,' she answered, just as quietly.

Anger swelled inside me, warring with guilt. I may have saved two lives today, but four girls had their souls stolen because of me. But Vronti and Arketa didn't know that. Why did they have such a problem with Titans?

'That's twice today I've been told *my kind* are evil. But I don't know what you're basing this on. Icarus saved Kiko's life. And I would never have let you, or Alexander, die today,' I said as calmly as I could manage.

She stared at me, and I stared back.

'I'm sure you have your own twisted reasons,' she said eventually, and turned over in her bed, putting her back towards me.

I let out a bark of frustration and rolled over in the other direction. *Fine*. Let her think what she wanted. I clearly couldn't win. And I was so very, very tired.

They made us wait three full days before we got our exam results. I was let out of the infirmary after I had awoken from a crazy long sleep, then we were all given two days to ourselves, other than dorm chores. I spent most of the two days talking to Nix about ways to catch death demons or reading books about manticores. I was praying that Neos was true to his word and knew what to do to catch the demon, because Nix only had knowledge on how gods could stop demons, which wasn't much help. All the research I was doing didn't distract me fully from the anxiety of our impending results though. We were allowed to fail only one class, and I was so nervous about history and language. I thought that geography and magical objects had gone OK, but the thought of wandering the world alone was keeping me awake at night all the same. What would I do if I failed?

As we sat in our seats in Dasko's classroom, Zali squeezed my sweaty hand.

'We'll be fine,' she whispered. The teacher began handing out papers, and it felt like a million years before he got to me. I half snatched them from him, flipping through them fast without even looking at his face.

Pass, pass, pass, pass.

I let out a massive sigh. I'd done it. I'd passed them all. I looked at Zali, who was beaming.

'I passed them all too,' she said. I hugged her, happiness oozing through me for the first time since I'd opened the box. At least *something* had gone right.

Suddenly a scream pierced the noisy chatter filling the classroom. I turned, releasing Zali to look for the source of the noise and my blood turned to ice in my veins.

Tak was rising from his seat near the front of the class, his body limp. I only half heard Zali scream beside me as I leaped to my feet, scrambling to get to him. He hovered in the air for a moment, then crashed back down, onto Dasko and Icarus who had beaten me to him.

'Call Chiron!' shouted Dasko, lifting Tak and moving him to the front of the classroom where there was more space. I pushed my way through the pale faced students gathering around him. Roz was kneeling by his unmoving body, tears streaming down her cheeks.

'He was so nervous and distracted this morning I-' a sob interrupted her whisper. 'I think he forgot to take his potion.'

I felt like somebody had punched me in the gut. *No, no, no, please no*. I struggled to draw in air as I dropped to my knees and gently pushed his hair back from his face. His eyes were completely black.

The next hour was a daze. We were herded back to our dorm rooms by the teachers, and Tak was taken to join the four girls the soul snatcher had already attacked. Zali hadn't uttered a word, and I didn't know what to say to her. I didn't know what to do, what to think, how to live with myself. I was too angry, both with the demon and myself, to cry. Frantic panic warred with a refusal to believe what had happened every time I thought of Tak's laughing face. Those black eyes... Bile rose in my throat every time I saw them. *What had I done?*

A knock on the dorm door startled me as I sat on my bed, legs hugged to my chest, thoughts spinning out of control. I looked at Zali but she just stared back, her expression hollow.

'We need the manticore feather,' Icarus said, as I opened the door. He pushed his way into our room and sat down hard on my bed. I stared at him. 'We need the manticore feather, now,' he repeated. 'How long until the fire rafe is ready?'

'Now,' croaked Zali. 'It's blooming from now until tomorrow.'

'Good. I have an idea.'

'I- I thought you didn't want to trust Neos and make his potion?' I stammered. Icarus's piercing green eyes met mine, and they were fierce.

'We don't have any other choice now. Between the three of us, we may be able to fight him, if we need to.'

I turned to Zali.

'Are you up for this?' I asked her.

'I didn't understand everything you just said, but if it means helping Tak, I'll do anything,' she said, standing up.

'We may have to fight. Demons.'

Zali narrowed her eyes.

'I just aced all my exams. I can fight just as well as anyone in this school. Even two all-powerful Titans.' My heart swelled with admiration and I wrapped my arms around her, squeezing hard.

'I know you can. You're the best friend I could possibly have,' I whispered. She squeezed me back and hope surged through me.

'So are you,' she replied. 'We can do this.' I let go of her and the determination in her expression mirrored my feelings. I turned to Icarus.

'What's your idea?'

. . .

We decided that Zali should go and collect the fire rafe, and Icarus and I would try and get the feather. I was worried about Zali going by herself, especially after the shark incident, but she was a mermaid shifter, who could communicate with sea-life. She'd likely do a much better job than me of looking after herself underwater.

'I really, really don't think he's going to agree to this,' I whispered to Icarus as we crept down a hallway in the boys dorms.

'Then you'll have to persuade him,' he answered, shortly. I could see he was no more thrilled about this plan than I was, but he was right. It was the best shot we had. When we reached the right door I took a breath and knocked.

'Pandora?' Thom said, surprise on his face as he opened the door.

'Hi,' I smiled. 'I need to ask you a really big favor.'

'Oh. Um, come in,' he said, opening the door wider.

'Actually, could you come with us?'

'Us?'

'Yeah.'

'So this isn't a date then,' Thom said with a grin.

Icarus coughed loudly and Thom's grin slipped as he noticed him standing in the shadows on the other side of me.

'No, no it's not. It's really important though. I think you can help the people who've been attacked.'

His expression became serious and he stepped out into the corridor.

'Then of course I'll come. Where are we going?'

. . .

'You can't be serious,' Thom said as we stood on top of the elemental building, where shifting class was held. 'Do you have any idea how dangerous this is?'

'But if we don't try then we can't help Tak and the others. I *need* a manticore feather.'

'So all that interest in manticores... It was just about this?' His voice was laced with disappointment and I tried to squash my guilt.

'Actually, I do find manticores fascinating,' I told him. It was the truth. 'But right now, I need you to shift into one, so I can get a feather.' I gave him my best pleading smile. I heard Icarus shuffle his wings behind me.

'Pandora, I have no control over myself *at all*, when I'm in that form. And you can't just pluck feathers from a manticore. I might kill you!'

'Just manacle yourself like you always do and let me worry about the feather. I won't get close enough for you to hurt me, I promise.'

He stared at me for a moment.

'Why do you need the feather?'

'It's for a potion I believe will help us stop the death demon.'

'Will it bring everyone's souls back?'

'No. But it will stop it taking anymore. And *then* we can work on getting back the souls.'

Thom took a deep breath.

'OK. I'll do it.' A surge of relief and adrenaline pulsed through me.

'Thank you, thank you,' I breathed.

'Gods, I hope you know what you're doing,' he muttered, shrugging out of his shirt.

So did I.

When we were sure his ankle was secured in the manacle, Thom gave me a final nervous look and told me to get
back a few feet. I gave him my most reassuring smile and
retreated across the rooftop. Icarus stood behind me,
watching apprehensively. Thom closed his eyes and tilted
his head up. There was an unsettling rippling across his
body, then in a flash a snarling manticore took his place,
his back haunch surrounded by the manacle. His dark
eyes locked on mine and I scanned them for any trace of
Thom. I saw none. My attention moved to the big red
wings protruding from the lion's body. His scorpion tail
was raised up and over his back, between the wings, as
the breast growled and pulled against the manacle. *One
feather.* I just needed one feather.

I called my water power, focusing on the pool below
us. After a second, long swirling ribbons of water crested
the edge of the building, flowing towards my outstretched
hand. I flicked my fingers, and the watery ropes changed
direction, aiming for the manticore. His cat eyes flicked to
the water ropes and he lifted a massive front paw and
batted at the first one to reach him. The rope fell apart,
the water splashing to the ground. I swore as manticore
Thom snarled and the manacle rattled as he tried to
move towards us again. I called more ropes up from the
pool, concentrating. I needed them to be solid, like they
had when I'd used them to pick the underwater mushrooms. I tried again, focusing every ounce of energy I had
on sending the water at the wings. This time, when the

manticore batted at the rope, his paw went straight through and the rope held. A smile tugged at my lips but I stayed focused as the ropes made contact with his left wing. There was a roar and the creature began to beat its wings hard, sending the ropes flying. I managed to keep them intact though, weaving around the beast now leaping and biting at the water. If it weren't for the brutal fangs and shiny stinger he would have looked like a kitty chasing a toy. I waited carefully for my moment, and as soon as there was a heartbeats lull in the manticores frenzied movement, I struck. One of the ropes darted down, to the bottom of the wing and I wrapped the end quickly around one of the lowest feathers. With a tug I yanked the water rope back to me. The manticore bellowed, so loudly I winced, then he rippled in front of us, and Thom was crouched on the rooftop, shirtless and panting.

'Ow!' he said, standing. 'That hurt!'

'But it was worth it,' I beamed at him, as the water rope above my hands dissipated and the leathery red feather dropped into my open palm.

24

We had agreed to meet Zali at the changing rooms, and Thom had insisted on coming with us, once we released him from his manacle. Icarus was still glowering about it, but I figured it was only fair. I mean, he had played an important part after all. We sprinted to the changing rooms and waited anxiously, until Zali burst through the door, dripping wet in her swimsuit. She was holding the most beautiful plant I had ever seen. Although it was green overall, red and orange lights shimmered up and down the long grass like stems, and each one was topped by a flower that phased through every color of fire.

'You should see it underwater,' Zali breathed as we all gaped at the plant. 'It's incredible.'

'It's pretty good here,' muttered Thom.

'Do you have the rust?' Icarus asked, turning to me. I nodded. 'Then let's go and find Neos.'

. . .

Zali and Thom didn't know Neos was involved, as every time we'd talked about him the Titan language had taken over. So they looked as confused as Neos looked delighted when we knocked on his office door on the mezzanine level of the front temple. He glanced at them both, then looked between me and Icarus.

'You two made up then,' he said with a lazy smile.

'We've got the ingredients,' snarled Icarus.

'Excellent,' he answered, and his eyes flashed scarlet. 'Do come in.'

'Dora, are his eyes red?' Zali whispered as we all followed Icarus into the office.

'Yeah,' I answered.

'Is he... not a normal teacher?'

'No,' I shook my head.

'Is he human?'

I shook my head again and she gulped. His office was plain and gave no sign at all that anyone spent time there. A large wooden desk like Chiron's dominated the space but there was just a small stack of papers in the middle of it. There was nothing on the walls and the bookshelves that lined the right wall were empty, save one or two simple black books. Neos gestured at the desk.

'Let me see,' he said. Zali stepped forward, laying the fire rafe down on the desk. I stepped up after her, laying down the manticore feather and the tiny vial of rust.

'And the blood...' I held out my arm. Icarus stepped forwards at the same time Thom said,

'Blood? What in the name of Zeus is going on?'

'Oh, nothing to do with Zeus, I assure you,' grinned Neos. 'We need much more space that this. And if you're all going to be present, you'll need to be ready for a fight. Do you have everything you need?' He looked at all of us in turn, his red eyes ablaze with life. We all nodded. My stomach was twisting itself into knots. 'Good. There's something I need to get from Chiron's office. I'll meet you on the roof of the elemental building in a few minutes.'

'What do you need?' I asked. Neos locked his eyes on mine.

'If you want to catch a demon, then you'll need a box to put it in. And I happen to know of just the one.'

My muscles clenched involuntarily as I thought of the box Chiron had confiscated when he'd found it empty by the pool last semester. The box I should never have opened.

'Fine. Grab the stuff and let's go,' said Icarus.

'Do you have any weapons?' Thom asked as we raced through the main temple and out to the training ground. With everyone still confined to their dorms we saw nobody.

'Yes. Two daggers,' answered Icarus, his wings streaming behind him as he ran.

'I don't,' I panted.

'Me either,' said Zali.

'I only have a slingshot,' he said.

'You can turn into a manticore. I reckon you'll be OK,' I said.

'And you can hit sharks with water. You'll probably be alright too,' he answered, looking sideways at me with a smile. Icarus suddenly flexed his wings, and without a word took off, soaring up towards the roof of the fast approaching elemental building. 'I'm getting the impression that he doesn't like me,' Thom said.

'Mmmm,' I answered.

The three of us took the spiral staircase up to the roof and I saw Icarus was standing at the corner, looking towards the main temple. With a deep breath, I made my way towards him.

'Someone might see you there. Your wings stand out, you know.'

He took a few steps away from the edge, then turned to me slowly.

'I understand, you know. He's a nice guy. And funny too,' he said quietly.

I stared at him.

'Understand what?'

'You and Thom. But don't let it get in the way of saving Tak.'

'Me and Thom? There is no me and Thom!'

'I see the way you flirt. It's obvious,' he said. I was both annoyed that he had assumed I was interested in someone else and so very relieved that he cared.

'Icarus, there's nothing between me and Thom.' I took a step towards him and gulped. 'I've missed you. So much.'

He raised his head, his beautiful green eyes boring into mine.

'Really?'

'Yes. Every day.'

'Why didn't you tell me?'

'You said you wanted time! And whenever I saw you, you either left immediately or seemed so uninterested. Half the time you wouldn't even look at me.'

'Because if I looked at you... I missed you even more.'

My heart fluttered in my chest and my breath caught. Was he really saying what I had longed to hear for weeks?

'Dora, I thought at the dance... I thought you'd be happier with Thom. He's so much less... complicated than me. And probably way more fun.'

'Icarus, I don't think having a boyfriend who turns into a lethal animal would be less complicated than dating you. And anyway, I don't want to be with anyone else! I have so much fun with you. You were going to take me flying.'

His eyes were softening as I looked at him, the hard lines on his face easing.

'I've got better. I reckon I'm strong enough to carry you now,' he said quietly, a smile tugging at his soft lips. A thrill ran through me at the thought of soaring through the sky in his arms, those huge, beautiful wings beating around us.

'I'd love that,' I breathed.

'Me too.'

. . .

'Let's catch ourselves a death demon!' Neos's voice sliced through the moment, loud and inappropriately cheerful.

'This will be over soon. And then we'll go flying,' Icarus said, and warmth spread through my whole body as he stepped forwards, taking my hand in his. 'Let's get Tak back.'

Neos had a frenetic energy about him as we laid all the ingredients out again on the rooftop. It reminded me of the way fire felt when I wielded it, excitable and unpredictable. And dangerous. He placed the box down on the roof, and I felt sick when I saw it. If I'd just left the stupid thing alone... As if hearing my thoughts Neos turned to me.

'If you hadn't opened it, I'd still be stuck in there, you wouldn't have any power and he wouldn't have those.' He pointed to Icarus's wings. Icarus narrowed his eyes back at him.

'Let's get on with this,' he growled.

'Um, did you say you'd be stuck in there?' Thom's voice came from behind us.

'Indeed, young man. Pandora here made a judgment call last semester,' Neos answered, and I closed my eyes, shame and guilt crashing over me. 'She opened a box Oceanus sealed a long time ago. And out popped a death demon. And me.' He flashed one of his wicked smiles, his red eyes roaring to life. Thom looked at me.

'Is that true?' he whispered.

'She didn't know what was in it,' Zali said, at exactly the same time Icarus said,

'It wasn't her fault.'

I didn't think I could be more grateful to them but I nodded at Thom.

'I opened the box and let out the demons. And I'm so, so, so sorry. But I'm going to fix it, I swear. We're going to catch it now, and then Neos is going to help us find a god who can convince Hades to return the souls.'

'I knew it. I knew it!' a female voice seethed and my stomach lurched as Arketa appeared at the top of the spiral stairs. 'I knew this was your fault.' Tears were streaming silently down her face. 'Kiko was taken because of you, you rotten, twisted Titan scum!'

'I'm sorry, Arketa,' I said desperately. 'I'm going to fix it, right now. This *will* work. We'll get her back.'

'It will. This is the best chance we have,' Zali said softly. 'Help us.' I snapped my head to my friend. Help us? There was no way Arketa would-

'What do I have to do?' Arketa snapped, and my mouth fell open as she strode across the rooftop towards us. 'You think I'm going to leave something this important to you lot? You must be joking. I'm getting Kiko back, no matter what.' She looked even more fierce than Zali had, her eyes hard under the tears. I believed her.

'Nice to have you with us,' said Neos, his arms folded over his chest. 'The more the merrier, at this point. How did you know we were here?'

'I was sneaking out to visit Kiko and I saw you, running here,' she scowled.

'What do we need to do?' asked Thom quietly.

'Mix up this potion, and then wait for the Keres demon. You've all taken your safety potion today, yes?'

We all nodded.

'Good. When it gets here, the potion will make it visible. You just need to get it into the box.'

'How?'

Neos shrugged.

'Up to you. What are you all good at?'

'Are you not going to help?' I stared at him incredulously.

'Yes, I already told you. I'm going to tell you how to make the potion.'

'What about the demon!'

'Oh, *I* can't catch demons. I *am* one. That would be against all our codes.'

Icarus gave a bark of frustration.

'I told you we couldn't trust him!' he snapped.

'Now now, wing boy. You can trust me just fine. Two Titans, a manticore and a couple of demigods should be able to take down a Keres demon. Just use what you're good at.'

Indecision raged inside my head. What if Icarus was right? What if Neos had planned this whole thing just to get us both wiped out in one move by the death demon? And I'd brought along my best friend, Thom and now Arketa? But if Neos was telling the truth and he had faith that we could defeat the thing... We had no other options. We had to try.

'If anyone wants to leave now, that's fine. This is my mess and I need to fix it,' I said, loudly.

'I'm staying,' said Icarus.

'I've already told you I'm staying,' hissed Arketa.

Zali gave me an annoyed, *don't be stupid* face.

'I want to help,' said Thom, lifting his chin.

My heart swelled with hope as I looked around at them all. I wouldn't be alone.

'Great. Whose blood are we using?' asked Neos, clapping his hands together.

25

I held my breath, wincing as Icaus's knife pierced my skin. It had to be my blood, this was my burden. But Icarus had insisted that nobody else took a dagger to me.

'Sorry,' he whispered as blood welled up in the little knick he'd made in my fingertip. I smiled reassuringly at him.

'It's already stopped hurting,' I said.

Neos appeared over his shoulder, holding a plain ceramic cup, shaped like the goblets from magical objects class. Icarus took it from him.

'How much do I need?' I asked him.

'Just a few drops,' he answered, and Icarus held the cup under my hand. I squeezed my finger, watching as three or four drops of the red liquid hit the bottom of the cup. 'Excellent.' Neos said, then turned back to the items laid out on the rooftop.

'Now add the rust,' he said. Icarus handed me the cup and then bent to pick up the tiny vial we'd stolen months ago. As he pulled the stopper from it, Neos inhaled deeply. 'You've done well here. The wearer of this armor suffered a violent death indeed.'

My stomach turned as Icarus poured the little vial into the cup. A small sizzling sound came from it and I barely resisted the urge to lift the cup closer to look inside. 'Feather next. Pandora, you need to get this one.' I handed the goblet to Icarus and picked up the feather. 'Now burn the feather so that the ash falls into the cup,' he instructed.

I held the feather over the goblet and called a tiny fireball. As carefully as I could I lit the end of the feather it had taken me so long to get on fire. It burned slowly, the smell unpleasant, and ash falling like dust into the cup.

'Good. Fire rafe last. Crush it, then tear it up and add it in.' It felt wrong to destroy something so beautiful, but I reluctantly crushed the flame-like flower in my fist, then tore the petals into little pieces and dropped them into the goblet. A steady stream of smoke was rising in a thin wisp from the concoction now.

'How long will it take for the demon to come?' asked Thom.

'The armor rust was strong, so not long at all,' Neos said. 'Heat the cup,' he said to me. I took it from Icarus and concentrated. A ring of fire appeared around the base of the goblet. The ceramic seemed to glow a faint red as it heated in my grip.

'Do we need to manacle you?' Zali asked Thom. He nodded, and then ran over to help attach the metal restraint to his leg.

'How will you fight or get away if you need to?' I asked him.

'I'll shift back to human and undo the chain,' he said.

I looked at him doubtfully.

'Are you sure you won't be safer untethered?'

'No. Definitely not. I'll be as likely to attack you as the demon in that form.'

Smoke was now billowing from the cup I was holding, and it was swirling around me in fat ribbons. Suddenly, I felt cold. I found Icarus's eyes across the rooftop and he shook his wings out behind him. Then Neos let out a bark of glee.

'Put the cup down on the roof!' he shouted, and I did as he said, gratefully. Immediately, the smoke leaped from it, thickening instantly and totally engulfing us. All I could see was Neos's glowing red eyes, facing me through the haze. The smoke didn't choke me, like I would expect normal smoke to, instead it felt more like mist, light but tangible on my skin. It smelled like iron and fire. Adrenaline rippled through my body as I heard a high-pitched keening sound. I pushed my senses out, feeling for the ocean, drawing on its strength.

'Dora?' I heard Zali's voice hesitant voice through the smoke.

'I'm here,' I called back, looking in the direction I thought she was. There was a snarl, and I moved cautiously, suddenly aware that I could no longer see if I was within reach of Thom. I also realized, with a start, that I could no longer see Neos's glowing eyes. Where was he?

The keening sound dipped in pitch, and I froze as a

shadow appeared in front of me. The cold I had felt earlier settled fully over me, my skin feeling like it was too tight for my body. Fear gripped me and before I'd realized I'd summoned it, water was swirling around both my hands. I raised them towards the shadow.

'Little Titan,' a voice hissed. It was like the sound of a sword being unsheathed, a slicing, awful sound. 'Frightened little Titan.' The shadow was growing, approaching through the swirling fog. My heart hammered in my chest, sweat mingling with the water in my palms, my thoughts erratic and useless. Where was Icarus, and Zali? Where was the box? What in Olympus was I thinking facing this thing? *Why had I opened that box?*

There was a rustle and a thud behind me and I stifled a shriek as I jumped and heard Icarus's voice.

'It's me,' he said, and my hair lifted from my face as his air magic whirled around him as he stepped up beside me. The smoke didn't react to it though, heavy as soup.

'Two little Titans,' the voice hissed, the shadow rippling.

'And a mermaid!' I felt Zali on the other side of me as I heard her shout. A terrifying keening cackle came from the thing but was drowned out by a roar behind us. It was Thom, adding his voice to ours. Strength bubbled in my core. We could do this. *Together*.

Glowing green vines suddenly blasted from my right, reaching for the demon. As soon as they touched the shadows though, they withered and died, turning deep black and falling harmlessly to the floor. I heard a yell of frustration from the thick smoke. It was Arketa. The demon turned slowly in her direction.

'Try again, Arketa,' I yelled and raised my hands high. As the shadow began to move, the vines flew forwards again and I launched my water at them, willing it to wrap protectively around them. They did, and this time, when they hit the shadow, they stayed green and bright. Slowly, they began to wind around the shadowy figure.

'Find the box!' I yelled. 'Somebody find the box!' I heard Icarus's wings, then felt a blast of air as he took off. I added my strength to Arketa's vines, feeling the struggle of the creature beneath them. Its keening unearthly wail was getting louder. Suddenly it stopped struggling and fell utterly silent. Suspicion welled inside me. It wouldn't be that easy to subdue, I thought.

I was right. With a sudden blast of power it burst from our restraints, the force making me stumble backward. I heard Arketa yell, and was about to throw my power back at it when I realized it was solidifying. Terror, true and crippling took hold of me. Only fifteen feet in front of me now, the thing was like something from my worst nightmares. Wings three times the size of Icarus's framed the shapely body of a voluptuous woman. But everything about her was wrong. Her skin was jet black and leathery and covered in huge gashes and open wounds, her wings rotten and torn. Her face was twisted into a permanent, hideous scream and her glinting eyes were as soulless as she left her victims.

'Foolish little Titan,' she hissed as she came closer. Her gaping mouth didn't move as she said the words and for a heartbeat, I felt so sick with fear I could barely think. But a pulse of energy from the ocean rocked through me, clearing the fear and haze from my mind and strengthening my muscles.

'Now,' I shouted, and vines flew at the demon again. This time, as soon as my water coated the vines and they latched onto the creature I felt a blast of cold from beside me and they began to freeze solid, pinning the thing in place. Zali was freezing the water, I realized. The demon writhed and hissed as Arketa shot more glowing vines at it, and I covered them with life-giving water before they hit the rotten flesh of the Keres demon, Zali freezing them in place.

'Hold on!' I heard Icarus shout from somewhere above us, and I widened my stance, pushing more energy into my magic. Wind began to whip at my hair, then a human sized tornado descended into the smoke. There, in the middle of it, I saw the box swirling around and around, moving closer to her.

She roared when she saw it, a guttural animal sound, and I felt the vines inside the water slacken for a moment. It was all she needed. The ice made a sharp cracking sound as she burst free, launching herself upwards with her great, hideous wings. Fear for Icarus shot through me and I ran towards the tornado. I reached out, grabbing the box from its center and looking up, desperate for a view of the Keres demon. I felt a massive burst of energy and threw myself to the ground just before the tornado exploded, air blasting across the rooftop. I heard a grunt and then the keening cackle again and I rolled over. The smoke was gone, the tornados explosion clearing it completely. The sight of

Icarus and the demon wrestling in the air had me scrabbling to my feet, and I launched my water ropes at the massive wings of the demon. Arketa's vines shot up too, wrapping around her waist. Together we pulled, dragging her back down towards the rooftop, and the box. She clawed at Icarus, her gnarled hands refusing to let go of him as she dragged him down too. Then, with another unearthly roar, she threw him from her and he soared backward, a trail of shadows coming from his body. I screamed his name and was half turning to race towards his falling body when I heard Neos.

'No! You've got her, don't let go!'

My eyes flicked back to her thrashing, flailing form, Arketa's vines dragging her down towards the open box.

'I'll get him!' shouted Zali and I felt power flood my body as I heard the thud of Icarus hitting the ground. My water ropes tightened and sharpened, and I tugged the demon down hard, straight towards the box I hated so much. She shrieked as her outstretched arm touched it, then swirling shadows leaped up from it, wrapping around her, seeming to fold over her whole horrible body. For a heartbeat her twisted face and soulless eyes fixed on mine, then in the blink of an eye, she was sucked into the box. Arketa launched herself at it, slamming the lid down. At the same moment, I heard a scream from behind me. I turned from Arketa who was wide-eyed and shaking, and my world seemed to slow to a stop.

Icarus had landed on the rooftop right by Thom. Who was fully shifted, and had his manticore stinger raised over Icarus's unconscious body.

26

I blasted water at the manticore before I could think. It hit him square in the chest and he leaped back, batting at the solid jet. Zali darted forwards and ducked low, trying to get to Icarus, to pull him out of the way, but the manticore roared and faster than I thought was possible, ducked under my barrage of water and scooped Icarus's arm up in his massive jaws. He clamped them down and started to drag him across the rooftop, his wings trailing. I screamed as I saw the blood pouring from his arm and the manticore froze, blinking. Did he recognize my voice?

'Thom! Thom, it's me. Put him down, please,' I called, as calmly as I could, stopping the water and approaching slowly. It's grip on Icarus's arm lessened as it blinked again.

'Thom, the demon is gone. Come back to us now,' I said, as calmly as I could manage, my whole body shaking with worry for Icarus. The manticore slowly opened its mouth, the bloodied arm dropping to the ground with a dull thud. Nausea rolled through my stomach as I glanced at it.

'Come back to us, Thom,' whispered Zali. The manticore looked at her, crouched down, amber eyes huge and round. There was a rippling of light around him, then Thom was there in its place. Horror spread across his face as he saw Icarus.

'No, no, no, no,' he whispered, the color draining from him completely. 'Please, please tell me I didn't do that.' I was at Icarus's side in a flash, turning him over gently.

'You didn't knock him out,' I heard Zali tell Thom. 'Just, um, the arm bit.'

'I need something to stop the bleeding,' I said, a horrible numbness taking over as I stared at Icarus's deathly pale face. Zali pulled her sweater over her head and handed it to me fast. I didn't know if he'd survive the fall, let alone the massive wound, but there was no way a sweater was going to make a difference. I laid my shaking hand on his chest. I could barely feel his heartbeat, and it was too slow. *He was dying.*

'Move,' someone barked. My power jumped, anger and fear taking over as someone pushed me out of the way hard and I fell back onto my butt. It was Neos. He began chanting something, low and as foreign sounding as I'd ever heard, and I pushed myself back to my feet, water swirling around my hands in an instant.

'What are you doing to him?' I demanded, choking on the words. He didn't answer, continuing the chant. Reason pushed through my raging emotions as Icarus's whole body began to glow red. If he wanted Icarus dead, he just had to do nothing. No, he was *helping* him. I moved to his other side, dropping to my knees and lifting Icarus's head onto them, pushing his hair back from his forehead. Neos had his eyes closed, and his hands on Icarus's chest. The red glow was starting there, and emanating out, shimmering all the way to his wings. Tears were streaming from my eyes, falling onto his beautiful face.

'Please,' I whispered. 'Please gods, let him be OK.'

Neos rocked back onto his heels suddenly, letting go of Icarus's chest and letting out a long breath.

'He'll be alright, but it wasn't the gods doing. No point praying to them.' He fixed his eyes on mine, flames dancing in his irises. I tore my eyes from his, and as I looked down at him, Icarus moaned softly.

'Icarus?'

He didn't answer.

'He'll be unconscious for a few days. And that arm probably won't work very well for a while. But that fall broke his back. It would have killed him.'

'You saved him?'

'Yes.'

'Why?'

'I told you. Olympus needs Titans. You two can reset the balance.'

'Thank you,' I whispered, tears still spilling onto Icarus's cheek.

'The other teachers will be here soon. Let me do the talking,' he said, and sprang to his feet, the red fading from his eyes. I looked around. Zali had her arms around Thom, who was visibly shaking and pale. Arketa was standing a few feet from me, her arms wrapped around the box.

'Keep that safe,' I told her. She nodded. 'What happens now? How do we get the souls back?' I asked Neos, dimly aware of the clop of Chiron's hooves below us.

'Now, you need to find Oceanus,' he said.

'I just don't understand why it has to be so difficult,' I sighed. 'Why can't Hades just give the souls back if we give him his Keres demon back?'

'It doesn't work like that,' Neos said. We were all sitting in the infirmary, around Icarus's bed. Thom had received treatment for shock, and was slowly starting to look and sound more like himself. He'd barely spoken in the hours since the rooftop. Arketa was sitting on a bed, arms and legs crossed, her face a permanent scowl. There was no denying how much we'd needed her help fighting the death demon, and she didn't seem to be going anywhere now. Zali was sitting next to me, squeezing my left hand, whilst my right gripped Icarus's.

Neos had told Chiron, Dasko, Fantasma and the others that we had stolen the box from Chiron's office and baited the demon with it. He convinced them that he had stumbled across our rooftop battle just as we vanquished the demon forever, and destroyed the box. His cloaking magic had hidden it from everyone else's view, and Arketa hadn't let it out of her sight since.

'Maybe we could convince him,' said Thom.

Neos raised his eyebrows.

'You think you could talk to Hades, Lord of the under-world, most elusive and mysterious almighty Olympian god? You'd never even get close to him.'

'Doesn't Hermes work for Hades? Can't he talk to him?'

'Hermes isn't going to cash in favors for a few kid's souls. Olympians live forever. He doesn't care enough about a few mortal demigods.'

Zali bristled beside me.

'He gave us the potion and seemed angry the gods wouldn't remove the demon,' she protested.

'Because he cares about his reputation and this school. You know you're competing with the other academies?'

I frowned. I hadn't known that.

'Well what about Zeus? One of the souls is Astra, his descendant.'

Neos snorted.

'Do you have any idea how many offspring Zeus has? Unless he's in the mood to pick a fight with his brother, he won't approach Hades.'

'He might, if Vronti asked him,' I said.

Neos shook his head as a cold voice said,

'He's right. Zeus isn't interested.'

Everybody leaped to their feet as Vronti stepped into the little room.

'How long have you been there?' I gasped.

'Long enough. Did you really catch the death demon?'

I nodded, as did Zali and Thom. Arketa said nothing.

'Yes. But you can't tell anyone. We want to get the souls back as much as you do.'

He stared at me for a long moment, then his eyes flickered to Icarus's unconscious form.

'I went to Zeus. I asked him if he could get Astra's soul back if I caught the demon. He refused.' His eyes were hollow and hard as he spoke and my heart went out to him. I sat back down slowly, and everyone followed suit except Neos, who clapped his hands together.

'See? If you want Hades to listen, you need someone important enough for him to listen to. Who owes you a favor.' Neos fixed his eyes on me. 'Pandora, you can find Oceanus. If you free him, he'll be obligated to help you.' I couldn't help the little part of my mind that flicked the Nix and the promise I made him. Imagine finding a long lost Titan...

'How do you know he's trapped? He just disappeared all those years ago with Prometheus. Maybe he left on purpose and doesn't want to be found.'

'I was one of the last to see him. And I assure you, beings that powerful don't just disappear.'

'Who trapped him?'

'Zeus, I would imagine. He's the only one strong enough.'

'Then wouldn't I be risking Zeus's wrath if I found him and freed him?'

'The world has moved on. Those two need to work out their differences, for the sake of Olympus.' He was echoing Dasko's words. What was happening in Olympus? I wished my warm-eyed tutor was here now, assuring me that this was the right thing to do. But I knew what he would say.

'How do I find him?' I asked.

Neos's red eyes gleamed and a grin spread across his face.

'You need a ship. A ship crafted by the great Titan himself. It is so tightly bonded to him that it will seek him out, if his own flesh and blood is standing at the helm.'

I gulped. So it really *was* only me who could find him.

'Where's the ship?'

'At the bottom of the sea. One more test, set by Oceanus. Only a true descendant of his could raise it from the ocean floor.'

'OK,' I breathed. 'Where?'

Neos spread his arms wide.

'Aquarius was Oceanus's realm, long before it belonged to Poseidon. It's right here, little Titan, hidden centuries ago along with the box.'

Arketa stood up suddenly, lifting the box from the bed beside her.

'Let's go then.'

'Now?' I gaped.

'Yes. Why wait?'

Neos grinned as he stood up.

'I heartily agree,' he said.

'But what about Icarus?'

'He'll be fine here. You don't need him to raise the ship.'

Panic thudded through me. I *did* need him. I needed him to tell me this was the right thing to do.

'If Oceanus can help get Astra's soul back, then we're

doing this,' said Vronti. I looked between him and Arketa, memories of the way they'd treated me washing over me.

'This isn't your choice, either of you,' I said as fiercely as I could manage. 'You've made my life as difficult as you could since I got here for being a Titan, and now you both need my Titan magic.'

'And whose fault is that?' spat Arketa.

Ouch. I couldn't argue with that. I ignored her, looking at Vronti instead.

'I'm pretty sure you've tried to kill me a few times,' I said, my heart skipping as his eyes dropped to the floor. It *was* him.

'Zeus... Zeus asked us to make sure you didn't do well at the academy. He didn't want you to survive your first year.'

Neos let out a long, low whistle. Zeus, who trapped people in an eternal hellhole, didn't want me to live?

'Because I'm a Titan?'

Vronti shrugged.

'Did he want you to kill Icarus?'

'No.'

'So it was you who trapped me in the manticore pen? And set fire to the attic last semester?'

He nodded, not meeting my eyes.

'Me and Astra, yes. And all the other little accidents you've had here.'

Anger seethed through me.

'Why? Why does he want me dead?'

'I don't know. I didn't ask. It's difficult not to do what you're told by the Lord of the gods.'

I glared at him. I didn't buy that he didn't want to

carry out Zeus's commands. I knew he'd enjoyed tormenting me. But enough to try to kill me?

'I say, if Zeus has got it in for you anyway, maybe finding an all-powerful ally isn't such a bad idea,' said Neos.

My mind raced, trying to process what I knew. Tak's face, his eyes filled with that awful empty blackness blocked out the rest of my thoughts though. We had to save him.

27

I took a long, steadying breath as we all crammed into the hauler in the pegasus tower. All except Icarus, I thought, nervously. Gods, I wished he was with me. If I'd been told that morning that I would find myself heading to the top of the pegasus tower with Neos, Zali, Thom, *Vronti and Arketa*, to raise Oceanus's own ship from the depths of the ocean, I would never have believed it. When we reached the top, I walked briskly to the edge. The salt air filled my lungs and power crackled to life inside me.

'You'll need to push your senses deeper than you ever have before, little Titan. Oceanus made that box. Feel it. Absorb its energy, so you know what to look for,' Neos told me. Arketa reluctantly handed the box to me. I didn't want to touch the thing, but did as he told me. I closed my eyes and pressed my hands around the box, like Fantasma had taught me in magical objects. For a moment, I could hear the ocean, crashing and churning around me. Immense power, so huge it wrapped around the entire world flickered into my consciousness. It was him. Oceanus's signature. I pushed the box back at Arketa, opening my eyes.

'I've got it,' I mumbled, and stepped to the edge of the platform, looking down at the deep blue sea. Here we go, I thought, and my senses left my body, plunging into the waves.

I was immediately aware of the turtle family, a whole bunch of sharks, a pod of whales, all within half a mile of the academy. I ignored them, moving deeper. The garden beneath the academy glowed in my mind's eye, a humming fizz of life covering the underside of the slab. I moved down farther, the light beginning to fade as my consciousness merged with the water, that feeling of becoming part of it taking over. There were intermittent sparks of life around me, some as massive as a whale, some as tiny as a shrimp, and I ignored them all, sinking myself further into the dark depths. I reached out all around me, searching for that feeling of power, the sense of immensity. The darkness was becoming suffocating, the sparks of life fewer and fewer. My breathing felt shallow and strained, and I knew that the bodiless me that was sinking to bottom of the ocean didn't need to breathe, so it must be my real body that was struggling. A sense of danger was rising in me, a feeling of *wrongness*. I was too deep. But what if the ship was close? It *had* to be.

And then I felt it, pricking the edges of my senses. Crashing waves in the still blackness. Unbindable power, wrapping around the world and giving it life. I pushed myself down, the sensation drawing me in. Suddenly, color and light filled my vision. An ancient ship, rotten and broken, glowed on the ocean floor below me. I reached for it, launching my failing power towards it. I heard a shout, a real human shout, and blackness began to close in around me. My real body was losing consciousness, I realized. No, I was too close! I pulled desperately at the ship but it wouldn't budge, that feeling of colossal power too strong for me. *What if...* A wave of bone deep fatigue washed through me and the blackness closed in again. I focused on the glowing wreck of a ship, trying to drag my thoughts into place. Oceanus's power was part of the sea. *I* was part of the sea. Pulling against his power was wrong, I realized. With a last burst of energy, I opened myself to the ship's power, to *Oceanus's* power, like Dasko had taught me in the pool.

Life, pure and strong and incredible filled me. Power surged through me and I rose, swiftly, shooting up from the darkness, soaring through the sea. And then I heard Zali saying my name and I realized I was back, back in my own panting body.

'Dora! Dora, you're not-' her words cut off as I turned to her and I heard Thom shout.

'Look!'

I looked out over the ocean with everyone else, in time to see the ancient ship burst from a churning, swirling mass of water below us, the word *Tethys clear* on the prow.

Peto whinnied when he saw me a few hours later. I had hidden the rotting ship a mile away from the academy, but we needed to be on it and away before Chiron, or even worse - Hermes, could stop us.

'Hey boy. We're going on a little trip. And we have a passenger,' I told him. Thom helped me lift Icarus onto Peto's broad back, then went to find his own pegasus. Thom had said he wouldn't come initially, that he would be a danger to us all, but Zali insisted we could work on his shifting. He had recognized our voices and stopped his attack, and she convinced him that meant there was hope.

Vronti and Arketa were coming, whether I wanted them to or not. They were both powerful, and smart, and there was no denying I needed the help but they both hated me. The thought of us all being on that ship together was seriously unsettling. Neos wasn't coming. He said that it would send the wrong message to Oceanus, bringing a demon that he had trapped. That sounded highly suspicious to me, but there was nothing I could do about it. He'd saved Icarus's life, and for now I had no choice but to trust him.

As we touched down safely on the deck, I had no doubt he was telling the truth about the ship belonging to Oceanus. The ancient wood tingled with power as my red converse hit the planks, and it was almost over-whelming. The others touched down beside me, the deck easily large enough to accommodate five pegasi. Zali and Thom helped me get Icarus down and my nose wrinkled in disgust as we laid him down on the slimy, filthy planks. We took our saddlebags loaded with food, water, blankets and clothes off the pegasi and I bade a reluctant farewell to Peto. Much as I wished he could come with us, there would be no stables on board, and we didn't have enough food for ourselves.

'How do we steer?' asked Zali as they took off, looking around the broken ship distastefully.

'Someone needs to bond with it,' I answered. 'Me, according to Neos.' Remembering what I'd learned about ships in geography class, I strode over to the giant mast, looking up at the torn and tattered sails. They shimmered faintly in the light. I took a deep breath and laid my hand on the mast.

Oceanus's power swelled inside me, and an unbridled joy filled my whole body. I watched in amazement as the sails began to knit themselves back together, beginning to gleam as they billowed. I heard the others gasping and muttering and turned to see the rotten planks of wood repairing themselves, shining like they'd just been polished. A red carpet appeared out of nowhere, leading up to the quarterdeck at the back of the ship and a massive spoked wheel righted itself on its previously broken post. The rotten sea-weedy smell was fading, replaced with a crisp, delicious ocean scent. Within a few minutes, the *Tethys* was ready to set sail.

I tentatively asked the ship to go to Gemini, as it was the nearest realm where we could get supplies, and it rose slowly but surely from the surface of the sea. We rose higher, and higher, until swirling pastel colored clouds surrounded us as we stood gaping on the deck. Spirals of glittering dust flew past us, reflecting off the beautiful sails. Hoping the ship was going where I'd asked it, I set about exploring. My priority was to find somewhere comfortable for Icarus until he woke up. We found that there were three levels below decks, all accessible by haulers on each side of the ship, and one at the back of the quarterdeck. The first level had cabins with beds, a galley and an infirmary. We made Icarus as comfortable as we could in the largest cabin I could find. The next level down was filled with huge slingshot type guns that Vronti told me were called ballistas. The bottom one was a cargo deck, and I marveled at the number of crates and boxes filling the hull. Small round portholes let in less light than the decks above and curiosity burned inside me as looked around at the massive shadowy space. What could be in the cargo hold of a ship this old? The sound of footsteps froze me in my tracks as I wandered amongst the boxes.

'Guys?' I called. Thom was up with Icarus and Arketa had insisted on doing nothing until she'd had a bath in the cabin she'd claimed. And I'd thought Vronti and Zali were behind me. I turned around, and spotted them prising the lid of a waist high crate ten feet behind me. 'I heard something,' I said, jogging back to them. Vronti dropped the lid and strode forward.

'We appear to have a stowaway,' he said, purple energy crackling to life around his raised hands.

I frowned and stepped up next to him, squinting into the dark shadows of the hull.

'Who-' I said, but my words faltered as a figure stepped forwards, into the light. My mouth fell open.

'Mom?'

THANKS FOR READING!

I hope you enjoyed reading more about Pandora and Icarus's adventures!

The next book, The Jinxed Journey is available here!

Made in the USA
Middletown, DE
06 April 2021